sic

CAS LUTHMAN

Cas Luthman

Contents

Acknowledgements

To Dr. Leon Jackson and Dr. Catherine Keyser, for all of your support in writing, editing, and submitting my thesis to the Honors College;

To all the girls in Women's Writing Workshop and to the UofSC Peer Writing Lab team, for your encouragement through each step of the writing process;

To Mr. J.T. Ellenberger and Mrs. Amy Fitzgerald, for being the best high school English teachers I could have ever asked for;

And, lastly, to my amazing friends Emily Loehrke, Kirsten Fisher, and Liam Martin, for loving me and supporting me through all of my life decisions (the good ones, of course, and the not-so-good ones);

Thank you.

Preface

The world as we knew it ended in the spring of 2020.

I found myself moving out of on-campus housing, flip-flopping between my parents' house and my now-ex boyfriend's, working a summer camp where I was nearly certain I would contract the disease that would kill me, and hoping that one day everything could be normal again. My world was spinning faster and faster around me as case numbers rose and the death knell echoed across the nation. I'd had anxiety before, but the start of the COVID-19 pandemic felt like a perpetual panic attack. My mental health was long gone and there was a time when I sensed no possibility of its return. But it wasn't just me—it was everyone, every single person on the planet. We tried to regain our sense of self without being able to go to concerts or see friends or travel across state lines; without room in the hospital for any illness that wasn't *it*; without knowing what the future, if it came at all, would hold.

It was the COVID-19 pandemic that inspired my thesis project. The idea of a pandemic is terrifying, of course, but what I came to understand is that it was the fear itself that made us the sickest. Mental illness spiked along with the death toll and even contributed to it. Even now, as we convince ourselves things are returning to normal, there is a trauma in each one of us from the end of our world that will not leave us any time soon. We are all scarred from the times we felt anxious, depressed, hopeless, and alone.

This collection of interconnected stories is written in a universe where, rather than COVID-19, it is mental illness that ravaged the nation. Of course, we know this to be the case in our own universe, but within these stories much more light is brought to the mental health problems individuals face. The stories may sometimes feel too fantastical or speculative to actually take place in the world we know. That is one of the biggest faults of our society—that the very real emotions people have are not taken as seriously as they should be, that we are left feeling alone in our struggles when if we simply recognized them we would find community and solace in the people around us who, chances are, also struggle.

My story collection, though fictional, is based largely in reality. Each character is someone, somewhere. We are all someone, somewhere. We each have our own experiences with stress and struggle and mental health. And together, we can find the hope and the love that will heal us.

SIC

The Circuit

Every front door tells a story.

On the corner of Blossom and Magnolia, the white door full of window panels tells the story of a young family. Kids raced around the halls, screamed, fought, cried, laughed. It is *the* door to stand at if you want a good show. The parents did their best not to make a spectacle of their little family, but the door was just the right prescription to help the neighborhood see everything that occurred inside.

That's how Nazira Adebimpe had been feeling lately--a spectacle for the world to see through glass. Each time she approached the front door of a house with a package or a stack of catalogs and letters for the mail slot, she saw herself, not only in the window reflections but also in the way the doors had been used, neglected. She was just doing her job, but that job took her to the doorstep of every household in every corner of the town, even in these trying times.

The Johnsons weren't doing very well since the start of the pandemic. It started with Mrs. Johnson, who fretted about every detail of everything in the home, since it was on display to the whole of the neighborhood, in addition to every detail of her three young children, who were a pandemic in and of themselves. Pandemonium, that's what

Mr. Johnson always called the household when he returned from his job at the Honda dealership. Nazira knew this only because her mail route took her to that house at exactly 5:17 every day, when Mr. Johnson got home from work. For years, their mail had been Toys-R-Us catalogs, congratulations cards for pregnancies and first communions, invitations to elementary school functions. Now Nazira brought them no congratulations, for there was nothing to congratulate. Mrs. Johnson had laid in bed for three months prior to her death, trying her best to stop wondering if the kids were learning everything they needed to, if her husband would get a promotion so they could afford a family vacation, if her mother would survive the pandemic. Mrs. Johnson never considered that perhaps her children would soon be learning to live without Mommy, that with or without a promotion there would be no vacation, or that hers was not the mother to be worried about.

Mr. Johnson was next to catch the disease, only a few days after his wife fell ill. He almost succumbed to it as well, when he became overwhelmed with grief from the loss of his love and then the added responsibilities of running the household alone. He was lucky his mother-in-law was able to step in to watch the children during the day. The eldest daughter looked just like her mother. Mr. Johnson's own parents made weekly visits with groceries, toys, and pre-cooked dinners. Sometimes the lasagna would arrive at the same time as the sorry-for-your-loss cards. That's how Nazira knew. That, and looking through the white door of window panels.

Nazira got only a glimpse of the world of each of the families on her route, but that glimpse, combined with the creative faculties of her mind, fabricated the full story of a household–its victories and failures, its dramas, its moments of love and moments of hate. For every home has all of those, and more, and to pass the time as she meandered the town in old Scar Face she found herself embedding her own person into the minds and hearts of the people to whom she delivered.

Scar Face was so lovingly named for the large scrape that once adorned the hood from an accident in Nazira's early mail carrier days (of course, it was quickly repaired for aesthetic purposes). It had been her closest friend for months, ever since she took the job. She worked long days and had little time for human friends. Less drama anyway, she told herself. Her miniscule social circle was her vaccination against the pandemic sweeping the nation. Nothing causes more anxiety than people all up in your business and you having to be all up in theirs. That's what Nazira told herself.

Every once in a while, Nazira found herself parked at the end of a driveway wondering what it might be like to have people up in her business. It had been a year since she had anyone who cared for her. It felt so long ago.

On this particular evening, Nazira found herself wondering why she worked so damn hard. What was the point? If her biggest fear was not completing her route by her definition of "on time," with no consequence, what was she doing? Perhaps a friend would be nice. But who was out to make friends at a time like this? *I hardly even see people going out anywhere anymore, let alone social scenes. Like this lady. I can't imagine her going anywhere--I don't even know if she is alive,* Nazira thought as she and Scar Face pulled up to a rusty brown mailbox.

The mailbox was so overstuffed with mail that the door wouldn't even close. Sometimes Nazira considered taking the mail up to the big oak front door--and sometimes she actually did it--but all that did was add another stack of unopened envelopes to the front porch's collection. For someone who never left their house, Ms. Solay sure received a lot of mail. The property teemed with letters from whom Nazira could only assume were daughters, cat-lover magazines, bank statements, clothing catalogs, and grocery store coupons. The bank statements made her think perhaps the old lady was alive. The unused, expired coupons made her think otherwise. Does your money still live when you are gone? Nazira had no time for questions like these, or to wonder what the letters said. As much as she loved to live the lives of others, it was approaching 6:00, and the Wongs did not like to be kept waiting.

Nazira and Scar Face rumbled up the long gravelly driveway to the home of the Wongs. They lived in what could be called a small mansion at the top of a grassy hill just outside of Ms. Solay's neighborhood. The mansion looked much smaller from the road, especially in the afternoons when the sun shone just slightly above and behind it, like a spotlight on the most beautiful and high-strung actress onstage, but upon her approach Nazira became overwhelmed by the towering white building, its many narrow windows, wisteria, and weeping willows giving it an antique yet whimsical look. The home had tall black doors, which might have been out of place if not for the recently-painted black shutters and black-tiled roof. Nazira only drove all the way up to the house because Mrs. Wong had sent a frustrated email to the post office complaining about having to walk all the way down the driveway to the mailbox to get her mail. Rather than explain that it was her own fault for living in that house, the postal service decided to have Nazira drive

Scar Face all the way up the drive and set the mail on the porch instead, ringing the echoing doorbell before her descent. Scar Face did not appreciate the extra workout, and grumbled about it all the way up and all the way down.

It seemed to Nazira that, in light of the pandemic, the post office would be a little lighter on its employees, not sending them up gravel driveways in old trucks. But her boss was clear--the point was to cater to the customer, especially when a customer has as much standing (and as much mail) as Mrs. Wong and her family. Sure, there would be bimonthly mental health screenings, as demanded by the higher-ups. The ones not climbing the hill.

The Wongs were well known in town--Mr. Wong was a successful attorney, and Mrs. Wong sold hand-stitched purses and wallets online. Their eldest son, George, was all set to be valedictorian of his class when he graduated and was also his high school's star athlete, bringing home a win in a number of basketball games and tennis matches. Their younger son, Vincent, may not have the grades and athleticism of his brother, but he was an extraordinary programmer and also ran his own small business fixing computers. The youngest Wong was a girl, Lily, sweet as can be and an incredible ballet dancer. Every team she was ever on won every competition it ever competed in. And she was only in eighth grade--physical and virtual newspapers alike always marveled at her potential to be even greater as she grew older. They were the family every other family wanted to be, the Wongs.

The Wongs' mail was always in abundance in the back of Scar Face. Sometimes Nazira wondered why they didn't just hire their own personal mail service, with all the mail they got and all the special requests they made. They received at least one decent-sized package every day, most often addressed to the Mrs. but not always. George got letters from colleges practically begging him to attend, or so Nazira assumed. Everyone knew what they thought was everything about the Wong family, but Nazira often wondered what happened behind those big black doors. It seemed the Wongs had little to worry about, but neither the media nor the mail could ever tell someone's full story. Did Mr. Wong grow stressed from work? Did Mrs. Wong ever get bored with how much she stayed home? Did George feel overwhelmed by all of his activities? Did Vincent feel he could never live up to his parents' expectations, or his brother's standard? Did Lily ever buckle under the pressure of her family's rising fame? These are things the Wongs would never show to the media, things that would never escape those big black doors.

The family was too perfect. Nazira knew there must be some form of darkness within the mansion's walls, and took it upon herself to create it in her mind. Everyone suffers from something. For Nazira, it might have been loneliness, if not for her truck. For the Wongs, it could be anything.

Down the street from the Wongs lived the Corbrums. When Nazira pulled up to their home at 6:18, she heard laughter from inside and couldn't help but wonder how much of it was forced. One of the Mr. Corbrums was actually a Dr. Corbrum, a hospital psychiatrist. Nazira didn't want to imagine his life, with all of the pain and suffering he experienced every day. The other Mr. Corbrum was a nutritionist.

Nazira's stomach growled as she pulled away from the Corbrum house. When was the last time she'd eaten? She looked forward to the leftovers waiting for her in her refrigerator at home.

Far from the Wongs and Corbrums, Nazira found herself, as per usual, entering the "bad part of town" around 7:00. She didn't mind Hazelwood Street and its surrounding dead-ends as much as other mail carriers, since she lived there herself. Her brother lived there too, once. Back before the start of the pandemic, Harold had been staying with a friend of his while he was struggling to make ends meet. That friend was one of the first deaths in town from the pandemic, but it wasn't big news to anyone outside that neighborhood. Harold came shortly after. Nazira had done her best to support her brother in those beginning months, but it didn't take long for life to take its toll.

Hazelwood was full of similar stories of poverty-turned-death even before the official start of the pandemic, and that year things had only gotten worse. The little church that once churned out Gospel music and hope was typically vacant, as was the run-down grocery and almost every house in the area. There were only a few houses that still received mail, and nearly all of it had some kind of bank or government seal on it. Nazira wondered how long it would be until the neighborhood was completely empty. She wondered if anyone would notice.

When Nazira had finally finished her route and arrived home at precisely 7:24, the chipped golden "314" on her apartment door was glowing in the light of the evening sunset. It was a solid metal door with no window and a large handle with an even larger lock. Behind the door was her dark, chilly apartment. She wouldn't need to turn the light on to know that the kitchen was immediately to the left and the refrigerator all the way at the back; to know that on the middle shelf of the refrigerator, just behind the coffee creamer, would be a tupperware of leftover spaghetti just waiting to be put in the microwave for one minute and fifteen seconds; to know that there were no forks in the drawer so she would have to get one out of the dishwasher that rarely worked; to know that the cheap bottle of wine on top of the fridge was half empty and would soon be slightly emptier; to know that there was no one on the couch to greet her, no one freshly showered from the bathroom to ask how her day was, no one in the bedroom to hold her that night. She would go the rest of the night without flipping a single light switch; she knew so well where everything was in her apartment and knew so well her routine that she might have done it with her eyes closed.

She didn't need light to know that she would return home from work, alone; eat dinner, alone; drink a glass of wine, alone; go to bed, alone; and then get up the next day to do it all again.

She didn't even need to open the front door.

A New Age

Penelope Ainsley Harris was born in a barn.

No, not like the sweet baby Jesus was born in a manger because the inn had no room, though she would grow up hearing that story at least once a year for her entire childhood. Penelope was born in a barn because her father was a farmer and he was milking the cows when her mother went into labor, so her mother went waddling and wailing her way out to the barn to tell him to take her to the hospital, and then out popped Penelope, right into the straw. Fortunately, said straw was clean. A moment later and it would not have been, and she might have been born into a family of flies buzzing about their feast.

Penelope's birth may have been a surprise, but very few things in the rest of her life were so. Her mother was meticulous and enforced order so well such characteristics were forced upon her eldest daughter. By age five, Penelope was gathering eggs in her little wicker basket without dropping a single one. By age seven, she was helping Papa milk the cows--without wasting a single drop of milk and by eight she did the dishes all on her own so Mama could rest. By ten she was better than any babysitter her parents could hire for her four younger siblings, making bottles and settling disputes and reteaching the subtraction the elementary school just couldn't quite get through JJ's thick bowl cut. More than that, she was by this time chief assistant to her Sunday school teacher, a straight-A student, and as much of a contributor to household funds as she could legally be thanks to her frequent lemonade stands. At eleven she learned to sew and by fourteen she stitched most of her own clothing, which eventually were passed on to her four younger sisters--for the girls and the three boys she knitted hats and scarves and mittens, and for her parents she made potholders as well. She was diligent, resourceful, and organized, just how her mother made her.

Puberty was more kind to Penelope than it is to most young girls. She was already prepared when the blood first came, and the breasts grew slow and steady, so much so that it was hardly a noticeable growth until age 16--she was still Penelope through all that time, more than just her body. Her hair had always been long and pretty but experience and wisdom taught her to keep it tame, tying it into tight buns that let no hair dangle free until she was 17 years old, when *it* happened.

When Penelope met Owen Solay, she knew she was looking at the boy who would become the man she would marry. Captain and quarterback of the high school football team, he was larger than life, at least in their little town. All the players looked up to him, all the students were jealous of him, all the boys wanted to be him, and all the girls wanted to be with him. So Penelope hatched a plan to win him over, and it started with a loose strand of hair twirled seductively around her finger on the sidelines of the big game.

Owen lost the game that night.

They were married at 20. Both of them went to college, Owen for business and Penelope for meteorology. Both graduated at 22, and their first child, Laney, came along at age 24. Kathryn didn't waste any time in showing up to annoy her big sister, though by ages 3 and 4 the fight for attention subsided and the two girls became best friends. Owen and Penelope were both so proud of their girls, though Owen didn't see them often because he was away for work. Penelope barely worked at all--she didn't have to, and she spent far more time thinking about her girls and her knitting than she did her career. She enjoyed sewing doll clothes and playing dress-up far more than she ever enjoyed reporting the weather.

As the girls got older, the dress-up turned to dress-shopping, which Penelope loved even more. She of course had a passion for making clothes herself, but she could easily appreciate a well-crafted article of clothing, and her girls could easily appreciate Daddy's credit card. Laney's piano recitals, Kathryn's plays, and both girls' school dances provided ample opportunity for Penelope to splurge on her daughters. When it came time for Homecomings and Proms, she was more than happy to indulge the girls in anything they desired--"anything" usually meant pink dresses to model, sparkly shoes to kick off five minutes in, and dangling earrings to twirl. But the weddings, oh, the weddings. Those were Penelope's favorites, not only because Owen retired early and was able to participate fully but also because she got to see her daughters as full grown women who turned out exactly as she made them: strong, beautiful, near-perfect women. Her own mother would have been proud.

After the graduations and the weddings, Penelope felt a little bored in life, even with Owen there to love and care for and all of the vacations he planned for the two of them. She went back to her old news station and was the weather girl a couple days a week, and on the other days she knitted winter gear for the homeless. She never missed a Sunday at church, and was active in the church choir as well as any community service projects the church undertook. The soup kitchens were her favorite because sometimes someone would come in wearing a hat or scarf she'd made. She liked knowing she made a difference in someone's life--that she mattered.

In life, Penelope had been a meticulous girl, a loving wife and mother, and a compassionate member of her community. In the purgatorial pandemic, she was still excessively careful but essentially nonexistent to all but her cat, as if she was already deceased. In death, it was the diseased Penelope who was remembered, more isolated than ever, more dead than alive.

One day, a 66 year-old Penelope Solay sat down on her well-loved brown sofa--it had once been slightly less loved and slightly less brown--with her cat and a framed photograph of her deceased husband to watch the morning news. It was a day that began like any other: earl gray in her favorite mug early on a bright sunny morning, fluffy white Athena curled up on her lap, her husband's memory sitting on the arm of the sofa beside her, the young meteorologist she had trained a year before describing a storm that would be rolling into town some time in the next couple of hours. With the sun shining so aggressively that warm May dawn,

Penelope could hardly believe a single drop of rain would fall on the day, let alone a whole storm.

"Amateur," she said, looking at Owen's picture. "I bet she's wrong. It's so nice out today--I'll probably have to water the roses later."

Athena meowed.

"Oh, now, don't you get going. I already fed you this morning."

The cat meowed louder.

"Oh, alright. I'll go see if there's any ham or turkey in the fridge. Just for a little snack. Just this once."

Penelope eased herself off the couch to move into the kitchen and Athena's white paws pitter-pattered behind her. The old woman could hear the swishing of a long white tail on the tile floor. It would not be just a little snack, and it was not just this once--both of them knew this.

When Penelope and Athena rejoined Owen's photo on the sofa, the weather report had ended and a different person was on the screen. He was sitting in an office at a desk by himself rather than at a table with other reporters, which was unusual for this station. Across the bottom of the screen, a headline: "A New Age of Anxiety, says Dr. Ethan Cassidy." Penelope rolled her eyes. Not this again. For the past week the morning news included a short segment on the deterioration of mental health in the U.S. Normally she ignored these reports and at this point in the day began watching game show reruns, but something about this man--perhaps the starkness of the single doctor alone at a desk grabbed her attention, or perhaps she was worn down from constantly changing the channel--something made her stay.

"..the numbers keep rising," Dr. Cassidy said. "More people every day are reporting excessive sweating, headaches, increased heart rate, shallow breathing, panic attacks, and spiraling thoughts. When untreated, some people have even begun to report signs of depression as well, such as loss of interest in regular activities and a lack of a will to live. If you or someone you know are experiencing any of these symptoms, don't wait. Go see your doctor, your therapist, your friends. Keep your connections strong and open. Keep yourself informed enough that you know how to take care of yourself but are not overwhelmed. Don't work too hard and avoid any mentally strenuous activity to the best of your ability. It may seem difficult to find the right balance, but it is more important than ever that you do so."

Penelope pulled her phone out of her skirt pocket. Laney and Kathryn had insisted for years that she get a smart phone despite their mother's insistence that she would never learn how to use it. After fumbling around with her passcode--Owen's birthday--she hunted down the green phone icon and her eldest daughter's name.

"Mom?"

"Hi, Laney. Have you been watching the news?"

Laney's sigh was just barely audible over the phone. "No, Mom, I haven't really been able to. Henry's been screaming since four o'clock this morning, and the girls have been demanding repeated showings of *Cinderella* for...you know, about the same amount of time. I don't even know what time it is--oh, gosh, I have to get Kayla ready for her doctor's appointment soon. Why, what's up?"

"They're still going on about this anxiety thing. I don't understand what the big deal is."

"Well, I talked to my therapist about it when I was there last week, and she said that as long as I remember to take care of myself I should be fine. I'm supposed to be talking to the kids about it too, teaching them self-care and to recognize their emotions and whatever, but I was kind of doing that already. They all seem fine for now. I think it's the same thing for you--just keep taking care of yourself. And if you need anything, call." A piercing shriek. "Sorry Mom, I gotta go. Maybe I should take Henry to the doctor too-- see if they have any time to check him out. This screaming needs to stop."

Penelope laughed, thinking about the days when Laney screamed like that and repressing her longing for them. "Alright, I'll call your sister. Let me know how the appointment goes. I love you."

"Okay, I will. Love you too, bye."

Penelope took a moment before pressing Kathryn's name. She stroked Athena's slinky, furry back, eliciting a loud purr. She then looked at the photo of her husband, missing him more than ever. Owen would understand all of this jibber jabber on the news. He would tell her not to worry about it, that he would take care of them. All of them. Athena climbed on to Penelope's lap and pawed at her stomach for more attention.

Athena had been Owen's gift to Penelope for their fortieth wedding anniversary. She had been lonely since the girls moved away, and though both her and her husband were retired, she still found herself wanting for attention and affection. Owen just couldn't bring her the same joy that raising her daughters had, and he knew that without her having to tell him. She had lost some of her spark. So he made some excuse about needing to get gas and left the house the morning of their anniversary, returning half an hour later with a white box tied with a pink ribbon. Penelope opened the box to find her new best friend, a little Persian kitten, cute and lively just like her girls had been. No one knew about the cancer growing in Owen's bladder at the time, or that it would spread before it was caught, or that he would only live for a year and ten days after the presenting of the gift. Athena barely got to know him because of all of the hospital visits, but Penelope knew him well, and loved him.

The phone rang.

"Oh, hi Kathryn! I was just about to call you."

Kathryn's smile was so infectious, Penelope could practically hear it. "Hi Mom! I figured you were watching the news. That doctor-guy was kind of ominous, huh?"

"Yeah, a little. I don't really understand what's going on. Why all the focus on mental health all of a sudden?"

"It's been a long time coming. I think that's part of the problem, that we've waited so long to address it. But what do I know, I'm just a theater teacher." Kathryn said something of the sort every time she was on the phone with her mother, because someone said something of the sort to her a few weeks earlier and she had yet to move on from it. "Anyway, I was looking at the CDC website, and cases really are climbing. They're calling it a pandemic now and really encouraging people not to be stressed, which is kind of difficult when you're telling them they're in a pandemic, but that's fine, I guess. I'm gonna start doing yoga in the mornings before school with the other teachers. Brad and I also were talking yesterday and decided to sit down every night and talk about how we've been feeling through the day and some goals for the next day. What are you going to do to keep your mental health up?"

"Oh, I don't know. How is Brad doing with the new restaurant?"

"He's doing great! He's tired a lot just from working so much, but business has been good and we've already made a profit, so no real complaints. I think he's planning to adjust hours so he can get a little more rest time because of the pandemic. You really should consider taking some steps to keep your mental health up."

"Don't you worry about me. I wish the news would quit going on and on about it, but I'm doing just fine. Your sister, though, she's a mess with all those kids. I'm glad she is seeing a therapist."

Kathryn laughed. "Oh yes, she tells me all about those kids. Apparently last week Janice got into a fight at school and got suspended. But Andrea won her mathlete competition, so that's pretty cool, I guess."

"You and Brad ever think about giving me some grandkids?"

"Mom, I already told you we're both too busy for that. Maybe we'll foster or something when we're older. Brad *has* been talking about getting a hamster, though."

From there, Penelope's call with her youngest daughter became less about the looming anxiety pandemic and more about pets, Kathryn's work, and summer plans. Kathryn wanted to come stay with her mother for a week or two on her summer vacation, and Penelope was of course all for it. She missed her girls.

After the call ended, Penelope placed her phone on the coffee table and turned off the news. She'd had enough of that for the day. She then took framed Owen back to their bedroom to get changed into her mud-stained jeans, a t-shirt of Owen's, and her old tennis shoes. She pulled her thin gray hair into a bun behind her hair, leaving just a few strands loose as she walked out the back door.

Penelope's garden had been voted best in the neighborhood fifteen years in a row, and for good reason. It took up the entire backyard--once Owen realized his daughters would never be into football like he was, he gave up on playing catch and turned the space over to his wife. The first addition to the yard was a large trellis, hand-crafted by Owen and painted white and pink by Penelope and the girls. Then came the stone pavers, laid one by one from the small concrete patio to and through and around the trellis. Red, pink, and white rose bushes lined the pathway, separated here and there by small angel statues, and blue morning glories fell in waves down the trellis. In the back of the garden was a bird bath with a solar powered bubbler, and to the sides were weeping willows the previous home owners had planted, or the owners before them, Penelope wasn't certain. The patio was surrounded by red and yellow pansies and contained a wooden porch swing, hanging baskets of ferns and pink petunias, and a bright red hummingbird feeder Penelope always made sure was filled with sugar water. She loved her flowers and she loved her birds.

Athena loved the birds, too, which meant every feeder in the yard was suspended from a clothesline.

The garden was always buzzing with the activity of the birds, the bees, and the butterflies. This Saturday morning was no different. When Penelope walked out the door she was immediately greeted by a brilliant orange monarch--those had been Owen's favorite, and she always thought of him when she saw one--soon followed by a goldfinch and its friends flittering around one of the feeders above the watchful eye of Athena, who had slipped out the door just before it closed. Penelope looked up at the sky; it was bright and sunny, just as she expected it to be, and there was very little moisture in the air and absolutely zero clouds. She pulled the green garden hose from the side of the house out to where all the rose bushes were, giving each one a healthy drink before moving on to the pansies and the baskets.

"Penelope!"

If Penelope Solay and Lavinia Washington were fourteen years old, they would almost certainly be frenemies. Since they were both in their sixties (or maybe Lavinia was in her seventies? Penelope didn't know), they were simply friends who consistently got on each other's nerves. Just as Penelope had a habit of going out into her garden after watching the morning news, Lavinia had a habit of scaring off all the birds with her hollering approximately six minutes after Penelope and Athena began enjoying them.

"Good morning, Lavinia." Penelope did not turn from her flowers.

"Did you watch the news this morning? I've been watching it, and I think the whole thing's stupid. Young people these days just don't know how to tough it out like we did back in the day." The closer Lavina got to the white picket fence, the more Penelope wished they had put in those tall hedges Owen liked.

Penelope had finished her watering and turned off the hose. "Yeah, I watched it. I called my girls after and talked about it with them. They seem to be taking it fairly seriously."

Lavinia scoffed. "Of course they are. Sounds like a bunch of bull to me, but you know, those young ones eat it up.

That's how the government gets them to do its bidding." She was always saying things like that, and Penelope never really knew how to respond without starting an argument, so she nodded her head and said she needed to go inside to get some housework done. How Lavinia had never noticed that Penelope was always doing housework--be it vacuuming or laundry, multiple times a week--Penelope didn't know. But her talkative neighbor always just smiled and said, on Saturdays like this one, "See you at church tomorrow!" And that was that.

The seat of the wooden pew on the right side, three from the front, approximately three body-spaces from the aisle, was more worn down than it was when Penelope and Owen first started attending this church at age 19, but it still served its purpose, and Penelope still sat there even without her husband. She sometimes took his photograph to church with her, but that day she did not feel like receiving pitying stares from other members of the congregation. Owen didn't like to go every week, anyway--he always said God would understand.

The preacher that day was someone different than usual, a younger man as opposed to the older woman who had been preaching the last fifteen years. She had taken a few weeks off for her health, the man said. He talked about mental health for the entire sermon, which of course just about drove Penelope mad (and certainly drove Lavinia mad, but that's another story), but she listened politely through the entire thing, trying her best to understand what was said.

"...In order to help our brothers and sisters who struggle with anxiety, depression, trauma, or other mental distresses, we must first learn how to know someone is struggling," the man said. "They may be avoidant, or extra emotional, or they may complain of bad dreams or upsetting flashbacks. In these trying times that are coming upon us, we must also be sure to provide a safe space, physically, spiritually, and emotionally, for those we love. Do your research. Talk to each other. Love each other. And know that here we have a community of followers of Jesus Christ willing to love just as he did, to be free of judgement, and to build each other up in our lives. Amen"

Penelope Ainsley Solay died in her garden.

No one knew for two weeks, not because no one cared-- the opposite was true--but because it had been so long since anyone had seen or heard from Penelope that they just assumed she was doing her own thing.

It started with an aversion to Lavinia. As the days, weeks, months went on, Penelope decided that Lavinia and her relentless chattering was getting to be too much for her to handle. So she snuck outside at night, when the darkness would hide her, rather than in the morning, when the sun might as well have been a spotlight. She missed being able to enjoy her garden like she did before. She couldn't see the flowers she watered, couldn't see the trellis her husband so lovingly built. Rather than being pink, and white, and red, and blue, everything in the garden was the indigo of night, if anything at all. Rather than birds and butterflies, mos-quitos buzzed and moths fluttered about Penelope's ears. Penelope never stayed out long. Athena never went out at all because of the raccoons and opossums rustling in the bushes.

Church came to be too much as well, not only because of the risk of seeing Lavinia, but also because of the presence of every other Lavinia in town, going on and on about how everything is changing and everyone is weak. Penelope didn't want to expose herself to that negative energy. She thought about talking to her preacher about it, but the regular one never came back, and the new one was too...new. So she stopped going, instead favoring a live-streamed service on the smartphone she still really didn't know how to use. But sitting still on the sofa for the entirety of the service when she wasn't there to hear the choir's voices echoing throughout the church or to see up close the emotion in the eyes of the preacher made it feel pointless. She felt no closer to God on her sofa watching a church service than she did watching a game show, and the game show was much more engaging. But she still prayed, and she still believed. God would understand.

Laney did her best to call once per week, as per usual. She talked about Andrea, Janice, Kayla, and Henry, but not their father. She asked her mother about life and church and emotional things Penelope felt silly considering. So Penelope didn't. She answered her daughter's questions, but her responses were always short of something.

"Mom, are you *sure* you're okay?"

"Yes, dear, I'm doing just fine. You worry about you and the kids, not me."

Kathryn called nearly every day, just after the daily news ended. She ranted about the government and how people were responding to the pandemic. She insisted she wouldn't have any kids: "Laney has enough for the both of us." She asked her mother about life, the garden, and her mental health, how she was taking care of herself.

"I'm doing fine, sweetie. How is the restaurant doing?"

"It's still doing great, but Mom, I'm kind of worried about you living all on your own. You could always move in with me and Brad, you know. I talked to him about it and he would be more than happy to have you living with us. I think it would be good for you, and a lot of fun."

"I'm not on my own! I have Athena."

"Mom."

"I couldn't. You and Brad have your lives, and I have mine. I wouldn't want to be a burden on you."

"You wouldn't be a burden, Mom. Don't talk like that."

"Ah, well. I've lived in this house so long. Your dad and I put so much love into it. I can't just leave it. Besides, who would care for the garden?"

"You can have a garden here--as much of the yard as you want. And we can help you move the trellis. Brad's cousin has a truck."

"No, no. I appreciate your offer, but I'm staying here."

"When can we come visit?"

"Oh, I don't know. Whenever is fine. Just give me a few days' notice so I can clean up a bit."

"Has Laney picked a day yet?"

"No, not yet. She has to work around the girls' schedules, and little Henry. You know how it is."

Eventually Penelope stopped responding to calls from her daughters.

It wasn't that she wanted to talk to them--she did, really--she just never had her phone on her anymore. The more time she spent inside on her phone the more she found herself looking at news articles about the pandemic, and at some point she decided she just didn't want to know anymore. So she turned her phone off.

She unplugged the TV, too.

After neither daughter had heard from Penelope in two weeks, Kathryn showed up one day to see why her mom wasn't answering any calls or texts. She found Penelope lying on the sofa with Athena and that same framed picture of her father that she just wouldn't let go of. She thought her mother was dead, and cried when the old woman stirred and sat up to ask what her daughter was doing in her house.

The girls started writing letters to their mom instead of calling, since they now knew about the cell phone situation. Penelope would respond to the letters at first, but her responses were always short and gave little information about her wellbeing.

Then, one day, she didn't get the mail.

She thought that by going outside to get the mail she might happen to go outside at the same time as Lavinia or another neighbor (though that had not happened in months, since she went out in the middle of the night), and she didn't like the sounds of the night animals and the itching of the bug bites. She never had much to write, anyway.

Weeks went by without a word from Penelope. Not even the neighborhood security cameras had seen her in her garden at night. Not much could be seen in the garden, anyway, with how overgrown it was. It was clear she had not been outside in quite some time. What she had been doing, only the cat knew. But no one had seen Athena either, except for a few neighbors who glimpsed the swish of a tail in the window when they went on their evening jog.

Kathryn and Laney called an ambulance together, though they knew there was little point. They stood in the weeds under the trellis, dead vines hanging down from above, coiling around their heads. Flies buzzed incessantly around one particular spot, next to the biggest withered rose bush. A body curled up into a ball in the brush, clutching a framed photograph in its pale, shriveled arms. Gray hair tangled in the weeds. The eyes had been clenched shut, but the mouth was a public nursery for maggots. When the paramedics arrived, they hardly looked at the body before scooping it up into a body bag on a gurney and wheeling it away, out the side gate to where the ambulance was parked out front. The ride to the hospital was completely silent.

Day X

It was still dark out when Marisa's alarm went off in the morning. She groaned as she turned it off, but then rolled out of bed and into her fuzzy but worn purple slippers. In the dark she found her way out of the room she shared with Kai, who was still sleeping, and into the laundry room around the corner. She pulled all the towels out of the dryer and folded each one, then took the stack of clean, folded towels into the bedroom for Kai to put away when he got up.

Next was the kitchen. She went downstairs and cleaned the countertop with a Clorox wipe with one hand and unloaded the dishwasher with the other. She then swept up the crumbs that fell from the counter, the mess under the kitchen table, and the hair gathered around the trash can before pulling a pop tart out of the pantry and eating it cold. She checked the time on the microwave: 6 o'clock, time to spray down her hair with dry shampoo, brush her teeth, change out of her night shirt and slippers into her work clothes, wake up the kids so they wouldn't miss the bus, wake up Kai, Swiffer the hallway, and then, finally, head off to work.

There were always a few stragglers after the bell rang at 8:30, but for the most part Mrs. Marisa Johnson's first period eighth grade World History class had arrived. As the students settled into their seats, she flipped through January's district mental wellness guide to the breathing exercises section. She quieted down her students, and began to read through a guided meditation, though she put her own spin on it.

"Before we begin our day, let us all take a moment to close our eyes and reflect on the weekend behind us, the week ahead of us, and this present moment. Inhale slowly through your nose, noticing how your abdomen expands as your lungs fill with air." Marisa looked around the room and saw that most of her students were following instructions, and smiled. "3...2...1...now exhale slowly, like you are trying to blow on a dandelion without losing any of the fuzzies. Good. On the next breath, if you are still feeling tired or overwhelmed from last week, inhale more deeply; if you are feeling stressed or anxious about the week to come, exhale a little harder, blowing the fuzzies off your dandelion. If you feel nice and balanced, count to ten in your head for your inhale and exhale, and try to keep them even. Keep breathing, nice and slow, in and out." Most of the students inhaled and exhaled more powerfully on the second and third breaths. "As thoughts pass through your mind, imagine reaching out to grab the ones that make us happy, that make us feel important, and let the others pass. These are just thoughts, like clouds, and they will pass. The bad thoughts do not define you. Good. Now, on your next inhale, slowly open your eyes and get readjusted to the light of the classroom."

Marisa was unsure about the district's mental health policy when it first came out. She did not think her middle school students would take it seriously, and admittedly she herself did not put too much real effort into enacting the classroom guidelines within the pamphlet. But now, nearly nine months into the pandemic, she was grateful to have all of the breathing exercises, yoga poses, journal prompts, and project guidelines provided in the monthly handouts. Most of her students listened and followed along as she read through guided meditations and instructions, and she had received many parent emails about how much their kids were benefiting from regular mindfulness exercises.

"Today we are going to be talking about the Black Death," Marisa said once all of her students were back from the world of mindfulness. "I hope you all read Chapter 6 last night. Based on the reading, can anyone tell me what the Black Death, or Bubonic Plague, is?"

A tall, frizzy-haired girl's hand shot straight up, to no one's surprise.

"Yes, Damonica?"

"The Bubonic Plague killed about a third of Europe as well as some people in Asia in the 1300s." Damonica pushed her glasses further up on her face. "It was spread by fleas and rats on ships, and then spread to more and more people in trade."

Marisa nodded. "Excellent. Now, without going into too much graphic detail, can someone else describe the symptoms of the plague?"

A small, red-haired boy had his head buried in his book, his eyes running back and forth across the pages. When called on to answer the question, he said, "It says people got big boils on their bodies that...leaked? Leaked, uh...bodily fluids. Is that less graphic?"

The class snickered, but Marisa hushed them. "That will do, I suppose. Thank you Parker. It's hard not to be graphic talking about it, isn't it?"

"Bruh, that's nasty." The brown-haired boy leaned back in his chair in that way he always did that made Marisa think he would tip over at any moment. Sometimes, secretly, she wished he would.

"Yes, 'bruh,' it is nasty," Marisa said, eliciting laughs from a few of her students. "Sit up in your chair, Nathan, before you hurt yourself."

The boy begrudgingly did as he was told, but not without rolling his eyes and breathing unnecessarily loudly.

"Now, Nathan, can you tell us how the plague was spread, based on the reading?"

When Nathan didn't respond, Damonica piped up. "I can!"

"Yes, I know you can, but I asked Nathan. You can answer another question later." Marisa felt guilty when Damonica shrunk back into her desk, but kept her attention primarily focused on Nathan. "Well? You can look back in the book."

"I don't have the book," Nathan said, flipping his hair to the side.

There was a time when Marisa would have asked *why* her most difficult student did not have his textbook, or scolded him for so obviously not doing the reading or even trying to find out the answer. There was a time when she would have been visibly frustrated, perhaps even raised her voice a bit at him. That's what her own teachers would have done when she was in school, and, though she now hated to admit it, it was what she had done for quite a large portion of her experience as a teacher. In the past year or so, however, she had been receiving monthly training about *not* doing that--about extending grace to every student because you never know what someone is going through. Marisa understood that, and fully supported the policy...most of the time. There were days, however, when she felt unable to discipline students because of it. This particular Tuesday was one of those days. Still, she followed protocol, asking him to stay after class for a few minutes to chat. She let Demonica answer the question.

"By touch!"

"Yes, thank you," Marisa said.

Nathan rolled his eyes. "Show off."

"Mrs. Johnson?" A small voice rang out from the back of the classroom.

"Yes, Violet?"

"I've been thinking. The book said 20 million people died of the Black Death, and my mom is a nurse and she said there have been almost a million deaths from the pandemic just in the past year. Are that many more people gonna die?"

Some students looked panicked, with wide eyes, jittery legs, and quick-talking mouths. Others seemed wholly apathetic. Marisa remained calm, knowing if she didn't get control of the classroom, there was a chance of an outbreak. That was the scariest part of the pandemic, she thought-- simply worrying about it too much was a symptom.

"The Bubonic Plague, as you may recall from your reading, lasted five years. It has not yet been two years of our current pandemic, and we are nowhere near that number." She knew that with the way disease spread, multiplying itself in more and more people over time, that the number of deaths would keep climbing, but hope and protocol dictated not going into the details of how little scientists and governments actually knew more than was necessary. "Hopefully, if we all keep having our check-ins with the guidance counselor and taking other measures to take care of our mental health, the number of deaths will go down. We just have to keep taking care of ourselves and each other." She smiled in a way she hoped was reassuring. "That said, I think it's great, Violet, that you are drawing connections between the Bubonic Plague and the world we live in today. You've read about the Bubonic Plague for homework, and today I will go through a presentation on other plagues and pandemics throughout history. Pay extra attention to any that interest you, because for your homework tonight I want you to write a paragraph comparing and contrasting a disease we learn about in class to our modern pandemic."

After class, Marisa had Nathan stay behind. Once the rest of the class was out the door, she closed it--second period could wait outside for a few minutes. Nathan never moved from his desk in the back by the window. He had one dirty tennis shoe up on the desktop and both arms stretched behind his head as he once again tilted his chair back. As Marisa approached, she noticed he had not brought anything to class.

"Nathan," she began, taking a seat at the desk next to his, "you didn't have your book today, or your notebook, or a pencil. What's going on?"

He blew his bangs out of his eyes. "Nothing's 'going on.' I just don't want to be here. This class is boring."

She pretended to be unaffected by his words, though something inside her stung. "Is there something I can do to make the class less boring for you? Would you like something to fidget with, a yoga ball to sit on, or maybe some one-on-one tutoring before school to prepare you better?"

He scoffed. "Why would I want to be here *longer*? And I don't need your toys. I'm not stupid."

"No one's calling you stupid. I just want to make sure I am doing everything I can to meet your needs. We are halfway through the school year now, and you still seem to be struggling. I want you to succeed in my class. Is there anything you can think of that would help?"

"Yeah, quit making me show up. I want to go home."

"What's at home that you want to go back to?"

He shifted in his seat. "I don't know. My dog. My video games. My brothers."

Marisa asked follow-up questions about the dog, the video games, and the brothers. She learned that the dog was a nine year-old yellow lab named Daisy, who liked to play fetch with sticks in the backyard. She also learned that Nathan preferred video games that involved shooting and aliens, but he also sometimes played racing games with his brothers, aged five and eight, when their mom was too busy working to entertain the younger boys. Nathan didn't know where his textbook was--his brothers had built a fort in the living room the night before, and a lot of things went missing from his room in the process. He'd been playing *Destiny* and didn't notice until it was too late. And he didn't want to read about history anyway--the present and the future were more interesting.

"Here's what I want you to do," Marisa said, wrapping up their conversation, "I want you to, instead of writing about one of the plagues we talked about in class today, I want you to write about a future disease. Make one up on your own, and then based on the way we are talking about the pandemic today, write about how you think we would handle the one you imagine in the future. Okay?"

He rolled his eyes. "When am I supposed to do that?"

"Well, I would love it if you could turn it in by tomorrow, but you can have until the weekend if you need it. Does that sound doable?"

"Yeah, I guess so." He stood up and made his way to the door. "Thanks."

As the next class, seventh grade American history, was coming in, Marisa sat thinking while pretending to read about the Black Death from the open book on her desk. Had she done the right thing by changing the assignment for Nathan? Was it fair to her other students that he got to do something different, and had longer to do it? Her first instinct was no. This one kid being rude in class does not deserve easier pacing for school work than every other kid, especially when she knew other kids were struggling and just not expressing it the same way. Violet, for instance, was in the process of getting an IEP for her anxiety, and Demonica, despite her energy and passion for learning, was struggling to get enough food to eat each day because both of her parents were recently unemployed and she had six siblings. And that was just a couple of the kids who were there--sweet Raymond wasn't in school that day or the day before because his father was in the hospital. Part of Marisa didn't want to assign anything at all for any of her students. There was too much going on in the world for them to worry about a worksheet or a chapter reading. But then, with the extra meditations added into the day and absolutely no change in the teaching standards in terms of what needed to be taught in what amount of time, how would she cover all of the course content without assigning some of it as homework?

The nation was changing, that was certain--but Marisa saw little extra support given to teachers. Even the wellness guide was meant mostly for the benefit of the students.

Lunch for Marisa that day was a slab of "pizza," a small side salad with an overly large packet of ranch dressing, and a bag of barbecue potato chips. She thought about getting a muffin, too, but she didn't want to subtract another dollar from her paycheck. So she took her muffin-less tray over to the teacher table and sat next to Kathryn, who smiled and waved.

Just as Marisa was about to say hello, she felt her phone vibrating in her pocket. She pulled it out and looked at the screen. Jordyn and Beatrice's elementary school was calling. "Sorry, Kat, I've got to take this," she said as she accepted the call and slid off of the cafeteria table bench.

There was an older lady on the other end. "Hello? Is this Jordyn Johnson's mom?"

What did Jordyn do now? "This is she."

"Hi Mrs. Johnson, this is Margaret again." Margaret Fuller was the dean at Huckabee Elementary. "I'm calling to let you know that Jordyn will be spending the remainder of the day in ISS. She was caught stealing other students' books out of their hands and throwing them in the trash can. Ms. Gardener told her multiple times to stop, but she wouldn't listen. I was told the last straw was when she threw a student's special reading book intentionally into some yogurt that spilled in the trash, ruining a couple pages."

Marisa sighed. "Okay. Thank you for letting me know. Kai and I will talk to her about it tonight."

"Sounds good! Also, I wanted to let you know that, since this is Jordyn's tenth ISS this school year, any further disciplinary problems will result in out-of-school suspension."

"Out of school? So someone would have to come pick her up?"

"That is correct."

Marisa felt her heart pounding in her chest. "My husband and I both work full time--neither of us can come get her."

The polite smile Margaret wore was audible through the phone. "Well, let's not worry about that just yet. Hopefully it won't even come to that."

Marisa took a deep breath. "Yeah, okay, that's true. It won't come to that. Thank you again for letting me know about today."

By the time the call ended, students were leaving the cafeteria for their next classes. Marisa didn't get to finish her lunch.

Once upon a time, Marisa had always looked forward to Advanced World History at the end of the day, but the past month or two she was completely exhausted long before that class began. She pulled up the study guide on the projector as her students settled in. She started reading through it when she saw a brown hand shoot up.

"Yes, Omar?"

"Um, Mrs. Johnson," the chubby boy said, "we didn't do our breathing exercise."

She blinked a few times before registering what he was talking about. "Oh, yes, that's right. Sorry guys, just a second." She powered down the projector and opened up the mental wellness guide. "To the count of ten, inhale slowly through your nose, noticing how your abdomen expands as your lungs fill with air."

After school, Marisa headed to the science lab classroom, where the biweekly staff meeting was being held. She sat on a low wooden stool next to Kathryn Solay-Lorton, the theater teacher.

She set her purse down on the black tabletop. "Hey Kat, how's it going?"

"Not good, honestly. My mom's birthday is coming up."

"Oh, I'm sorry. That must be difficult."

"Yeah. It's like, I talked to her every day, and now she's gone, and I can't even call her on her birthday." Tears welled up in Kathryn's eyes, but she brushed them away. "Anyway, how are you?"

"I'm doing pretty okay, all things considered. Just the typical crisis of whether or not I'm being the teacher my students deserve, or if it's even possible to be a good teacher in these conditions."

"True!" Kathryn began to rant on and on about how inconsiderate school policies were of their teachers, and how the wellness guide, though well-meaning, simply wasn't enough, and how students were struggling and teachers were struggling and everything was the government's fault.

Marisa imagined that, as a teenager, Kathryn was one of the angstiest in her class. Probably an emo kid, like Julia, one of the seventh graders. Marisa loved listening to Kathryn talk, and she knew anger toward the school board was just the thing to distract her friend from the sadness of having lost her mother. It had been months, but Kathryn still wasn't quite over it. Marisa was lucky to have both of her parents still alive, though her mother's health was failing. She didn't yet understand what Kathryn was going through, having lost a parent to the pandemic, but she knew it was only a matter of time before she would. And regardless she wanted to be there for her friend. She did everything she could to support her, which often meant, in Kathryn's case, getting her riled up over other things.

The meeting that afternoon began with a breathing exercise similar to the one Marisa used to start her classes. Then the main topic came up: Behavior Plans. The district wanted more individualized plans for students, especially those with IEPs and behavioral issues. In addition, the plans needed to be not only thorough and detailed, but framed in such a way that no one could view the child, the plan, or the school in a negative light. The idea was to promote both positive thinking about the student's ability to succeed and overcome the issue. After passing out pamphlets, Principal Dunn began to describe their contents:

"As you can see in the pamphlets, the first step for our new behavior plans is to define the behavior we seek to change point-blank, and then reframe it using only positive terms. Maybe we have a student who yells in class. Instead of saying he needs to 'stop yelling,' we might encourage him to speak at an appropriate volume, and then define what that volume would be." He wiped his forehead with the back of his hand, and then continued. "Step two is to analyze why the behavior is occurring. What is the student's reason for yelling, and is he getting what he wants when he does it? If he is seeking attention, are you giving it to him? Is he getting it from his peers? Things like that. And then how can we limit how much of what the student wants is received? Step three is to implement the plan you come up with from steps one and two, and then step four is to re-evaluate the plan periodically to ensure that it is working."

Marisa thought all of this sounded great, but also that it sounded an awful lot like what all of the teachers had already been doing, except maybe the more positive language. She would have to try that, maybe with Nathan later in the week.

As Marisa and Kathryn walked out of the science lab, chatting about lesson plans for the rest of the week, scrawny Ed Vanderbilt, the aged life sciences teacher, hobbled up to them.

"Oh good, I'm glad I caught you," he said, pushing his glasses higher up his nose. "I wanted to ask a favor. Tomorrow I need a few of my students that are also in both your classes to retake a test tomorrow, and I was hoping they could come to my room during one of your classes."

Kathryn was visibly livid, her eyes wide and her cheeks the bright red of the fire extinguisher on the wall. "Absolutely not! We have a performance we are rehearsing for! And you can't infringe upon other people's class time!"

"What students?" Marisa asked, ignoring Kathryn's protests.

Ed squinted at a sticky note in his quavering hand. "Jamari, Desmond, Trista, Lily, and Nathan. All in eighth grade."

Marisa was not surprised to hear most of those names. Jamari wasn't a bad student--he was the lead in almost every performance the theater program put on since he had been at the school, and his grades were pretty decent--but sometimes his passion for theater overshadowed academics, particularly STEM courses. Desmond had been out of school for weeks because of the pandemic, and was just coming back, so he had lots of work to make up everywhere, though most teachers tried to limit it under the circumstances. Trista would probably never have to work a day in her life, and often got caught cheating on tests and quizzes. Lily, though very bright and a hard worker, sometimes missed school for dance competitions, making her a regular for make-up work. Nathan was no surprise at all. Marisa wanted better for him.

"I suppose that's fine. I can let Desmond, Trista, and Nathan out of first period a little early to start it, and then you can write them notes to be late for second--I think they all have Jenny for Algebra. Jamari and Lily are in my advanced class at the end of the day, so I will just send them to you--it's a review day, so they won't miss much so long as they read the study guide.

"Perfect, sixth period is my planning so I can let him test then. The others can sit in the back during my first and second period classes. Thank you!" He smiled. "And thank you for being reasonable, letting the important subjects come first." And he scuttled off.

Kathryn turned to Marisa with tired eyes. "The nerve of that slimy little man! You don't have to do that, you know. You can tell him no. I do it all the time. Really pisses off the math teachers because 'theater isn't even a real class' and all that. Can't believe he would lump history in there like that. You're a core class. You can say 'no,' no problem."

"I know, but I don't want to fight with him, or with anyone for that matter. I'm tired. We all are. We just have to push through."

Kathryn's eyes softened. "That doesn't sound like a healthy mode of thinking, at least not nowadays. Do you need some time off? I can cover your third period during my planning if you want."

Marisa smiled. "Oh, no thanks! I'm doing fine. Just the same amount of tired as anyone else." She looked down at her watch. "It's 5:00 already? I have to get going. See you tomorrow!"

Marisa's drive to Olive Garden was only ten minutes, but her shift started at 5:15, and it was rush hour, and she needed to get changed. She pulled off her flowy blouse and slipped her arms through the sleeves of the wrinkled black button-down on the passenger seat while she drove, grateful she had worn a tank top under her shirt that day. She shuffled around in the glove box for her name badge and glanced up at the mirror at every stoplight, trying to wipe the mascara from under her eyes and smooth out the frizzy parts of her wavy brown hair. Finally, she whipped into the parking lot and parked in the first spot she saw, then changed her shoes and stumbled inside.

Her manager Nirupa stood beside the hostess at the front. "You're late again, Mar."

Out of breath, Marisa replied, "I know, I know. I'm sorry. I had a meeting after school that went longer than expected."

"Let's come talk in my office," Nirupa said, kindly but firmly.

Marisa nodded and followed her boss through the kitchens to a narrow back hallway where a storage closet and the manager's small office were. She was nervous. This was the fourth time in a row she had been late.

The drive home was twenty minutes, though that night in particular it felt like an eternity. She had to stop for gas on her way–she always forgot to get it in the morning, and was, as per usual, running on fumes. As she pressed the *UNLEADED* button on the pump and put the nozzle into her car, she noticed that the family next to her was Nathan's. In the car was a tired looking mom in the driver's seat fussing at two young boys in the back, and Nathan was pumping the gas. However tired Marisa was, she was grateful that she had her husband and didn't have to go through life alone.

"Hi, Nathan," Marisa said, dredging up the little burst of energy she found in thinking she could be worse.

"Hi Mrs. Johnson."

"Have you had a chance to start that assignment we talked about?"

He didn't make eye contact. "Yeah."

"You don't have to lie."

He said nothing.

"I found out yesterday that you're in theater. How are you liking it?"

"It's stupid."

"Oh, now, don't say that. Why are you taking it if you don't enjoy it?"

He sighed, but gained some animation in his face. "My mom made me. She said I need to get 'more involved' in school stuff. I wanted to play basketball, but..." his voice trailed off.

Marisa remembered the week of basketball tryouts. Many of her students had been getting excited that week, and then when the Thursday of tryouts arrived, they were all anyone talked about. Nathan had been particularly talkative that day. Then, on the Friday after, while most of his friends were talking about getting new basketball shoes, he said not a word to anyone.

She decided not to keep basketball in the conversation. "Do you have a part in the play?"

"Yeah, I'm supposed to be Alfred Doolittle," Nathan said. "But I might skip the performance--Carter is the understudy, and he is way better."

"I don't know, you got the part, not him. Mrs. Solay-Lorton must see something in you."

"Maybe."

"Is Jamari playing the professor?"

"Of course."

"And who is playing Eliza?"

"Some sixth-grader. I think her name is Lauren? Or maybe Lacey. I don't know. She's really annoying."

Marisa laughed. "Well, she must be talented if she got the part that young. And, for what it's worth, I think it's really cool that you have a part too. I bet your mom is proud."

Nathan glanced behind him at his family's minivan. His mom was still turned toward the boys in the backseat. "Yeah, maybe." His gas pump clicked. "I have to go."

"Alright! Enjoy the rest of your night, and I'll see you tomorrow, Nathan."

Once he and his family had gone from the gas station, Marisa's own gas pump clicked that it was done, and she got into her own car to leave. When she finally pulled into her driveway at nearly 9:30, she could see through the storm door that Jordyn, Beatrice, and Eli were all still wide awake, and poor Kai, that sweet, loving man, was absolutely exhausted. Even from the car she could see the bags under her husband's eyes.

"Mommy!" the chorus of children exclaimed as Marisa walked through the door. They engulfed her in hugs and tugs on clothes.

Eight year-old Jordyn, always the tattle-tale, was the first to speak after the greeting concluded. "Mommy, Bea took my hairbrush again!"

"I did not!" Bea screamed, her pigtails swinging as she jumped away from her big sister.

"Did too!"

"Did not!"

Marisa sighed and looked to her husband, who discreetly pointed across the room, where little Eli had retreated behind the couch. She could see the end of a hot pink, sparkly hair brush in his hand, and she couldn't help but laugh.

"Alright, now, as I've said a million times, it's time for bed. We can solve the mystery of the hairbrush in the morning," Kai said with a smile.

Jordyn stomped her foot. "But Daddy, I need it *now!*"

"Jordyn, you're too old to act like that. You never brush your hair at night. You don't need it now. I bet in the morning it will be right back in your drawer." Kai winked at Marisa, who calmly went to get the brush from their three year-old son.

Marisa squatted down to her son's level. "Eli, baby, you know it's not nice to take your sisters' things."

He shuffled his feet nervously. "I didn't mean to make them mad. I just wanted to be pretty too." Tears formed in his eyes.

"I know baby, I know. But now we know better, right?"

He sniffled. "Yes Mommy."

"Okay. I'm gonna take the brush back to their room. Will you go get into your jammies and get into bed for me?"

Eli nodded and handed Marisa the brush, then ran off up the stairs.

Marisa returned to the hallway, hair brush hidden in her purse, which she never managed to get off her shoulder. "Now, girls, Daddy has said many times now that you need to go to bed. So go. Now."

Crying and stomping, Jordyn and Beatrice followed their brother up the stairs.

Before following them up to make sure the children actually went to bed, Marisa turned to her husband, eyebrows furrowed. "Kai, we've talked about this. Bed by 8:00 for the girls, 7:30 for Eli. What happened?"

"You saw yourself what happened," he said flatly.

She sighed. "Any word on that promotion at work? I almost got fired from OG today. One more strike and that's it, I'm done."

Kai frowned. "Unfortunately no. But I promise I'm trying, Honey."

"I know. I know." She leaned into her husband, who wrapped his big, hairy arms around her. "Have you heard anything about my mom?"

He held her tightly and rubbed her upper back. "Jack called a couple hours ago. She's still in the hospital, but seems relatively stable. Doctor said if she stays that way for 24 hours, she'll be able to go home."

"I wish I could be there with her." Marisa fought the tears trying to break free from her eyes.

"I know you do, and she knows, too. And so does Jack."

"I wish I hadn't used up all my sick days, then I could go see her."

"I'm sorry you had to use them to take care of me."

"No, no, that's not what I meant." The tears started flowing--Kai broke his wrist at work a few months earlier, and she had taken a little time off from both of her jobs to help him. "I'm sorry, Baby, I didn't mean it like that. I just...I'm tired." She sniffled. "I think maybe I should just go to bed."

Kai stroked the side of her hair to calm her, but Marisa could hear his heart rate increasing in his chest. "We need to eat first. Did you get anything today?"

"Oh, yeah." Marisa pulled away from her husband, wiped her eyes, and pulled a styrofoam box out of her bag. "Chicken alfredo. It's not a lot, but it should be enough for you."

"And for you?"

"I'll be okay. You eat tonight--I will get something for me tomorrow."

"Marisa, you need to eat." He placed his hands on her stomach. "For you, and for the baby."

"It's fine, really. You eat. I ate a couple breadsticks around 7." She moved to go up the stairs, but then turned back. "What did the kids eat?"

"Dino nuggets and green beans."

"Okay, good." She wished she could give them more, but anything shaped like a dinosaur was hard for them to complain about. The green beans, on the other hand, were not, but canned vegetables were better than nothing. "I'll see you in a bit. I love you."

"I love you too."

As Marisa climbed the stairs, listening to the giggling of her children who had suddenly reconciled, she allowed herself a small moment of peace. Or, she tried to. The pain in her feet from standing all day made peace difficult to attain. She was ready to sit down; to lie down in bed, warm under the covers; to rest.

Marisa was still awake when her husband came up to bed. It was 11:00, and she lay staring up at the ceiling in the dark. She wanted to go to sleep, but her mind wouldn't stop racing.

"What are you thinking about?" Kai asked as he climbed into bed.

She sighed. "I forgot to tell you earlier, but I got a call from Jordyn's school. She got in trouble again today."

"For what?"

"Taking the other kids' books and throwing them in the trash."

Kai collapsed into his pillow. "Fantastic," he said, sarcastically. "What do we do?"

"I'll talk to her in the morning. But you should know, she is done with ISS. If she acts up again, one of us will have to go get her."

"How are we doing to do that? We both work!"

"I know. That's what I told the school. They didn't really have an answer, just, 'hopefully it doesn't come to that.' But Kai, I'm really worried it will." Tears formed in her weary eyes.

He pulled her into a hug under the covers. "We will get through it. Whatever happens, we'll get through it. We'll have to."

She didn't remember going to sleep that night, but when her blaring alarm startled her awake, she got up to face the day.

Atychiphobia

Dr. Hugh Corbrum's early morning drive to work was his least favorite part of the day, but also the most important. The tone he set for himself driving to the hospital would affect his actions and mindset throughout the rest of the day. He cranked the music loud and rolled the windows down, blasting reggae as he passed by all the drive-thrus and department stores that cool November morning. He was grateful the heat of summer had left the city, and even more grateful for the lack of humidity that had been admitted from June through September. He loved the crispness of Autumn air.

"Good morning, Dr. Corbrum."

"Good morning, sir."

"Dr. Corbrum, good morning!"

"Up and at 'em early again, eh, Hugh?"

"Good morning."

Hugh had been well-known and liked at St. Dominic's before the start of the pandemic, but since then his popularity only grew. Every other doctor, nurse, and student in the building came to him for psych evaluations of their patients, and every patient who knew he existed insisted on chatting, just for a moment, about the state of things. He didn't really mind, except on the days when he had his own patients to attend to, which, by that point in the pandemic, was every day.

The first patient for him to check in on that day was Mrs. Laney Brinson, who admitted herself the night before due to suicidal thoughts.

"Good morning, Mrs. Brinson. How are you feeling today?"

The woman slowly sat herself up in her bed. Her brown hair was knotted and tangled, and she was just as pale as she had been when she checked in. "Eh, I don't know. I'm worried about my kids. I never should have left. I really should get back." She began to rise.

Hugh stood by the bed so she could not get out. "No, no, it's good you came in. You said yesterday your sister came to watch the kids, right?"

Laney sighed. "Yes, I did, but she doesn't have any kids, or really even want kids, and I would have much rather them go to stay with my mom, but she died back in June." She sniffled. "I hope Kathryn is getting them to school okay. And taking care of the house. I don't like the idea of her staying in my house."

"I'm sure everything is fine, but I understand why you would be worried about it. And I'm sure trying to cope with the loss of your mother hasn't made life any easier. Would you like to talk more about that? Or is there anything else that's been troubling you?"

"I mean, I haven't heard from Steve in, oh, seven months. But that's nothing new, and I've been talking to my therapist about it. That doesn't bother me so much any more. But my mom, and the way she just slowly faded out--it's scary to think that people can go out like that. And I miss her. Maybe I should've called more. Or maybe if I'd visited more often--"

"You can't blame yourself for what happened to your mom," Hugh said. "These are scary times we live in, and the best anyone can do is take care of themselves. It sounds like you've been going through a lot." He looked down at his clipboard. "Let's go through your medical history real quick, and then we can get you set up with some new medication and a new plan for therapy. What medications are you taking currently?"

Other doctors might have been worn down by treating suicidal patients first thing every morning, but Hugh was pretty well used to it, and that was where he found his passion. After his own failed suicide attempt back in high school, he discovered his calling in treating mental illness. No one would ever have to suffer like he did. Not on his watch. That said, he did feel for his patients. He just tried not to think too hard about it.

When Hugh returned home that evening, his husband Pablo was chattering away on the phone; he couldn't make out what exactly was said. As soon as Pablo saw him, he ended the call and embraced him.

"Hey, Honey, how was work?" Pablo asked.

Once released from the hug, Hugh shrugged. "About the same as usual. How was work for you?"

"Oh, you know, same old same old. I did get referred to a new client today, so that's exciting. Family where the mom and son have diabetes--Dad is looking for some healthy snack options."

"Ah, I see. Is that who you were on the phone with?"

"No, actually, I wanted to talk to you. Come sit," Pablo said with a smile. He seated himself on their worn leather sofa and patted the space next to him.

Hugh sat. "What's up?"

"Well, I just got off the phone with the adoption agency, and they said we sound like we would be great parents. Of course we will have to have quite a few meetings in person, and they need to talk to both of us, and you know, some people won't be very accepting of our family, but--"

Hugh's heart lurched in his chest, and his hazel eyes felt like they were trying to burst out of his head. "Adoption? Babe, we talked about this."

Pablo sighed. "I know, I know, but I thought maybe once we got the ball rolling you would change your mind. There are so many kids out there who need homes, and we have the money to do it, and I've always wanted kids. I just thought it would be a good thing to look into. I know you don't really want kids, but I wish you would give it a chance."

Hugh put his arm around his husband, ignoring the sweat beads rolling down his own neck. "Baby, you know it's not that I don't want kids. I just don't have time to be the father they would deserve. I'm almost always working, and by the time I come home, I'm completely exhausted. All I want to do in the evenings is curl up on the couch with you, like this. I don't want to have to take care of kids too--at least not right now."

"But when?" Pablo turned toward Hugh, his big brown eyes full of emotion. "We're in our forties now. I don't want to wait so long that I'm too old to play with my kids."

Hugh sighed and kissed him on the forehead. "I know, I know. There's just a lot going on right now. Can we wait until the pandemic is over?"

"But what if it's never over?"

Each tick of the big wall clock echoed throughout the living room.

"Well," Hugh said at last, "we can at least wait until people have adjusted to it better. Established a 'new normal,' you know?"

Pablo's eyebrows narrowed. "You always say there is no 'new normal,' that it's just something the media says to try to calm people down."

"You're right. I'm sorry--I shouldn't have said that. It was insensitive."

Pablo's facial muscles relaxed a little as he exhaled. "Yeah, okay." He stood up. "I'm going to the gym."

"Wait, please. I'm sorry Honey, we can talk about it more." Hugh gave a small smile and patted the seat next to him. "Please."

"No, I don't want to right now. Maybe tomorrow. I'll be back later, but I'll probably need some space."

"Okay. Take as long as you need."

"Yeah. Bye." The front door clapped shut. Then it popped open again and Pablo poked his head back through. "But you really have to stop with the excuses. If you don't want a kid, just say so."

Hugh sighed. "It's not that, you know I do, it's just–"

Pablo slammed the door before Hugh could finish his sentence. Hugh tried not to think too hard about it.

Long after Pablo had gone to bed, Hugh sat at his laptop at the kitchen table, a cinnamon-apple candle lit in front of him and a "Best Doctor" mug of Earl Gray by his side. The mug was a gift from the family of a child he helped a pediatrician treat for PICA a few years back. The little girl had been eating sand from the playground sandbox, and developed some gastrointestinal issues because of it. Ironically, the girl's name had been Sandy. She was the cutest little thing, with bright blonde pigtails and baby blue eyes the color of the walls of her new baby brother's nursery. She loved to talk about her stuffed-animal weddings, and how she hand-made the invitations. Hugh had been invited to one of them, for Mr. Barry B. Bear and Pinkie the Pig. Sandy leaned in close to him when she handed him the invite. "They are both boys," she had said with a smile. He regretfully declined the invitation, but she insisted he hold on to it. He still kept it pinned to the corkboard in his office.

Hugh scrolled through his social media page, and all he really saw were kids. Aunt Delilah went on and on about how much she loved her new granddaughter, who had just been born to his cousin Melinda and her husband Joel. Francisco from high school, now an engineer, had a daughter on her way to graduating college and another to graduating high school. Marisa from middle school now taught middle school herself, and often posted stories about her students as if they were her own children. Nurse Louisa's twin boys just started Kindergarten, and Kyla the HOA president had a son who won a spelling bee and a daughter who won a soccer game.

Hugh opened a new tab and pulled up the nearest adoption agency's website. Just for kicks, he told himself. He read through their process, their requirements. Researched costs of all kinds. Looked up the average amount of money needed to raise a child–it was a lot. He logged into his online shopping account–not the account he shared with Pablo–and looked at cribs, highchairs, and baby clothes, and then blocks, dolls, children's books, school supplies. Stuffed animals–giraffes were Pablo's favorite. "Best Daddy Ever" onesies and t-shirts and mugs. Train sets--those had been his own favorites as a child. It was all so cute, but it felt unreal, like some kind of fever dream not only for those items to exist, but for them to potentially exist in Hugh's home. And it was all so expensive!

He felt a hand on his shoulder and jumped.

"Baby, why are you still up? It's 2 a.m." Pablo rubbed sleep from his eyes.

Hugh abruptly closed his laptop. "Oh, I was online for a while and then got distracted and lost track of time. I'll come to bed now."

Pablo yawned. "Whatever. Do what you want. I shouldn't have even gotten up."

"Yeah, why did you even get up if you were going to come down here just to be in a bad mood?" Hugh asked sharply as he got to his feet.

Pablo's brown eyes glistened in the light of the candle. "I...I don't know. I'm sorry. Can we just go to bed?"

Hugh felt heat rising in his cheeks. "You can't come down here acting like that and then ask to 'just go to bed!' What's wrong with you?"

"I don't know." Pablo scratched the back of his head. "I just-" He sighed. "I wanted to apologize. For earlier. I shouldn't have called the adoption agency without talking to you about it first. I won't go behind your back like that again. I'm sorry"

With a single deep breath, Hugh's anger left as quickly as it came. He kissed his husband on the cheek. "You just got excited. I understand."

"I love you."

"I love you too."

Room 310: an elderly man with heart palpitations related to panic attacks. Room 311: a teenage girl overwhelmed by her AP courses who had hardly eaten in the past two weeks. Room 312: a young woman who passed out due to shortness of breath and choking sensations when she found out her dog was hit by a car. Room 313: Mrs. Brinson, who would only need another day of monitoring and talking to a therapist before she could return to her family with a new medication. Room 314: a man about Hugh's age who has struggled so much with concentration at work that he was fired. Room 315: a young man who had not slept more than two hours in three days. Room 316: a middle-aged woman whose husband claims she has been extra irritable lately. Room 317: a yoga instructor complaining of muscle tension. Room 318: a little boy who started acting out at school and at home. Room 319: a new mother who couldn't stop worrying about, well, anything. Room 320: a young man with severe agoraphobia. Room 321: a little girl with separation anxiety who screamed inconsolably any time her mother leaves the room.

There was a time when some of these patients wouldn't have been patients at all, at least not in a hospital. They may have gone to an independent therapist or psychiatrist, or even just their general health practitioner. But in the past few months more and more people had been admitting themselves and their family to the hospital for mental health concerns, and in light of the pandemic, every single one was required to stay at least one night. The hospital could barely hold all of its patients--the third floor wasn't even the psych floor, but the fourth floor was full and the maternity ward relatively empty, so there they all were.

Hugh didn't really mind the change of scenery. It gave him a reason to use the stairs, get a little more exercise. Pablo was always working out--Hugh never felt he had the time.

"Dr. Corbrum! Dr. Corbrum!"

Hugh turned around to see a frantic-looking young man rushing towards him. His hair was sticking up in all directions, and he had deep purple bags--no, not bags, more like luggage--under his eyes. "Hello, Mr. Taylor, how can I help you?"

"My wife," he began, panting, "how much longer until she's better? I can't handle the baby on my own anymore. It's too much."

"Just a moment." Hugh and Mr. Taylor walked to Room 319 and Hugh pulled the file out of the slot on the wall. "Let me see," he said, "it looks like she hasn't been showing much improvement. In addition to post-partum depression, her anxiety is through the roof, and we have yet to find a medication that calms her down without putting her to sleep. Still trying to figure out what the best course of action is." He looked at the man inquisitively. "Where's the baby?"

"I left him with a nurse while I came to find you. I needed a break."

"Okay. Let's go get your son, and then we can go see your wife. Okay?"

Mrs. Taylor had only been in the hospital for three days. Hugh worried that soon Mr. Taylor would need to be admitted, too, for his own anxiety and inability to properly care for himself. Yes, these things were common for new parents. But in the context of the pandemic, every shift in mood or habit was taken very seriously. What would happen to the baby if both parents were in the hospital? Hugh tried not to think too hard about it.

Hugh had just left the Taylor family when he was approached by a tall, blonde-haired woman in big sunglasses and a business coat. Ms. Ruby Peterson. Her orange complexion revealed that she had recently been to a tanning booth, and her red-orange cheeks revealed that she was quite upset about something.

"You." She pointed her manicured finger at Hugh. "Yes, you. Right there. *Where* is my daughter?"

"Rosamel is in her room as far as I know, Ms. Peterson. Why do you ask?"

"Because she isn't in there, *obviously*." Ruby eyed the name badge on Hugh's chest. "Geez, and you got a medical degree? Didn't realize they were just giving them away to any idiot who asked."

"Give me just a moment, ma'am, and I will locate your daughter," Hugh said calmly. "It's possible she was taken away for a test by one of her other doctors."

Hugh walked quickly down the hall to room 311, followed by Ruby's clicking heels. Sure enough, Rosamel Peterson was not in her bed. He entered the room and looked around. The sheets were tossed aside, the blanket was missing, and the wheelchair was still sitting by the side of the bed. The bathroom door was ajar, and no one was inside. Hugh exited the room and went to the nurses' station.

"Hey, Louisa." He lowered his voice a little. "Do you know if anyone has taken Rosamel Peterson out of her room for anything? Or have you seen her leave?"

The nurse twirled her pen in her thick black curls. "Hm, I don't know of anyone taking her or anything. My shift just started a few minutes ago, though. She must've left before then."

"So *none of you* know where my daughter is?" Ruby was fuming. "Pathetic. This whole hospital is pathetic. We should've never come. I don't know why she insisted on this anyway. She's always just looking for attention--that's what she's doing now, too, I bet. Hiding out somewhere to make her poor mother worry. What a brat."

Louisa came out from behind the desk. "Hi, Mrs. Peterson. Come with me to the waiting room for a moment so we can talk about when you last saw your daughter while Dr. Corbrum keeps looking for her." She threw Hugh a glance over her shoulder as she turned Ruby away as if to say, "you owe me."

As the two women walked away, Hugh went back to Room 311 to see if there were any more clues. For some patients, a disappearance would have been highly troublesome and warrant a full lockdown of the hospital. But he knew Rosamel, and was confident that she wouldn't run away or do anything to harm anyone. He was fairly certain she wouldn't harm herself, either, after all the work they had put into her mental health in the past few days. Hugh knew that a few days would never solve any serious mental health issues, but he also knew that Rosamel was dedicated to getting better. He believed in her. And because he believed in her, and because he had taken the time to get to know her, he had a pretty good idea of where she might be.

In the service hall behind the cafeteria, where the laundry room and many of the supply closets were tucked away out of sight of the patients, someone had painted a mural of a tree on the wall. Hugh didn't know who did it—it had been there longer than he had—but he knew it was beautiful. The tree had a thick brown trunk intertwining branches that reached all the way up to the ceiling. Leaves of all colors adorned the branches, shining brightly in the dim light of the hallway. It was here that Hugh found Rosamel.

"Please don't tell my mom I'm here." Rosamel was sitting on the cold tile floor, still wearing her hospital gown but wrapped in the thick blanket she'd been given the night before. "I don't want her to find me."

"I won't tell her. She's with a nurse right now." Hugh sat down next to his young patient. "It's a little chilly back here, hm?"

Rosamel nodded. "The blanket helps."

"I'm sure. It looks very warm."

"You don't have to stay here with me."

He smiled. "I don't mind. It's probably just about as cold back here as it is outside. Fall is my favorite season, you know. I like the crispness of the air, the way it stands out to all of your senses."

"Fall is my favorite season too. I like big cozy sweaters, and when my grandma makes pumpkin pie."

"Ooh, that sounds yummy." He looked down at his watch. "You know, it's just about lunch time. Do you want me to sneak out to the cafeteria and bring you something to eat? I think they have grilled cheese today, and let me tell you, the grilled cheeses are the best."

"Oh, that's okay. I don't want to put you through any trouble."

"It's no trouble, really."

"Ah, I don't know. That's okay."

"It will be really good, especially with some warm tomato soup."

"I'm okay, but thank you."

"Rosamel."

She looked up at him, eyes wide. "I'm not starving myself again, I promise. I just don't really feel like eating right now."

Hugh didn't feel the need to tell her that sometimes that's how eating disorders work--she knew that already. He dropped the subject for the time being. "So, why are you avoiding your mother?"

"Oh, the usual," Rosamel said flatly. "Since you left her with a nurse, I assume you're avoiding her too."

He laughed. "You got me there."

After talking in the service hall for a while longer, Hugh and Rosamel took the elevator back up to the third floor-- Rosamel couldn't walk very well, so the stairs weren't really an option. They snuck back into Room 311 and got her back into bed, tucked in snug under the blanket. Then Hugh took her lunch order--a grilled cheese sandwich and a small bowl of tomato soup--to the cafeteria before fetching Ruby and Louisa from the waiting room. He had to separate Ruby and her daughter within two minutes of them greeting each other. Sweet Rosamel would be in the hospital for a long time. Hugh tried not to think too hard about it.

When Hugh arrived home that night, the kitchen smelled strongly of cumin and chili powder. A baking sheet of cooked chicken breast sat on a potholder on the counter, and plates of warm tortillas, diced tomato, and shredded lettuce sat nearby. A bowl of sour cream and another of freshly-made guacamole occupied the center of the kitchen table. Pablo had always been a great chef.

"Hey, Honey, this all smells delicious." Hugh set his brief-case down in the entryway. "Thanks for making dinner."

"Of course! I'm glad you think it smells good, but just wait until you taste it--I really outdid myself this time, if I do say so myself." Pablo grinned. "How was work today?"

"Nothing too out of the ordinary." Hugh began setting plates and glasses on the table. "We had an incident with my anorexic teen, but it all got under control pretty quickly."

"That sounds so stressful," Pablo said, shaking his head. "I don't know how you do it."

"Same way any of us do anything, I suppose--following our passions."

Pablo rolled his eyes. "That's what you keep saying, but your job just seems so difficult. Especially emotionally. I could never."

"I bet you could. For me, it's really just about caring about people and wanting to meet their needs. You're pretty good at that."

"True as that may be, I would have never made it through med school." Pablo chuckled. "Gosh, I barely made it through undergrad."

"But you did!" Hugh squeezed his husband's hand as they sat down for dinner. "How was work for you today?"

Pablo shrugged. "Pretty boring, actually. I didn't have any appointments, so I mostly focused on organizing my diet sheets. I did vacuum the house, though, and I made dinner."

"Sorry your day wasn't so exciting. And thank you for taking care of the house. I appreciate you."

Pablo smiled and kissed his husband, then said, "Thanks Babe. I appreciate you too"

After dinner, Hugh did the dishes while Pablo put a load of towels in the washer. He always insisted on washing them separately--something about different temperatures, color bleeding, fabric softener--but Hugh liked to throw everything in together. That's why, early on in their marriage, he was banned from the laundry room. He could fold things on the couch, which he would do for the towels in a couple of hours, but he had nothing to do with the washer and dryer. He only found out recently they had an ironing board.

Once the dishes were done and the laundry was started, Hugh and Pablo sat on the couch together scrolling through Facebook on their phones. Hugh came across more posts about children. Good old Francisco was still proud of his daughters for all of their academic achievements. The younger one looked a bit like Rosamel--skinny, dark-haired, bright-eyed. Hugh wondered what Francisco was like as a parent. Was he always worried about his family, like the Taylors? Was he controlling and selfish like Mrs. Peterson? Was he angry and judgemental like Hugh's dad had been? Was he kind and nurturing like Hugh knew Pablo would be?

What would Hugh be like as a parent? He tried not to think too hard about it.

He pictured Thanksgiving dinner, Pablo poking the turkey in the oven and a little boy setting the table; Christmas morning, a handful of munchkins rooting through gifts under the tree while Pablo took pictures with his Polaroid; the night before Easter, Pablo stuffing plastic eggs with quarters and candy while the children slept; on a plane over summer vacation, a little girl pointing excitedly at the clouds while Pablo smiled sitting next to her; Pablo dropping the kids off for their first day of school, backpacks stuffed full of crayons and notebooks and glue; Halloween night, Pablo holding the hands of little girls dressed in hand-made fairy princess costumes. Hugh could easily see Pablo being the best dad in the world, the dad every kid wished they had. He couldn't see what kind of dad he would be. He tried not to think too hard about it.

"Hugh, is everything alright?" Pablo placed his hand on Hugh's knee and looked at him worriedly.

Hugh rubbed his eyes and found that his cheeks were wet. "Not really, no."

"What's wrong?"

"I wish you hadn't called the adoption agency. I'm not ready."

"I know. I shouldn't have done that. And I'm sorry I did. I won't talk to them again until we are ready."

"Okay."

"Do you want to talk about anything?"

"What if I'm not good enough?"

Pablo chuckled and shook his head.

Hugh sobbed.

Pablo pulled his husband into a tight hug and held him as he cried. "Is this what's been stressing you out so much?"

Hugh nodded weakly in Pablo's chest.

"You're plenty good enough, I promise. I laughed because the idea that you would be anything less than a fantastic father is absolutely ridiculous. You know that, right? Somewhere inside of you, you have to know that."

Hugh wiped his eyes. "What if I turn out like my dad?"

"You won't."

"But what if I *do*?"

"You won't–you can't. Your dad, he didn't have nearly the amount of love and compassion in him that you have in you. If we had a kid, you would love them like you've never loved anyone before. Give them all the love you wished you'd had."

"But what if I can't? What if I have too much of my dad in me?"

"Do you really think that?"

Hugh was silent.

"We are all a product of our time. For some of us, we become our parents. I see more and more of my mom in me every day, and if my dad was around more, I'm sure I would see some of him in me too," Pablo said. "But for others, for people like you, you learn from your parents' mistakes and you grow from them. You learn from them what not to do, and are better for it." The washer sang in the hall, indicating that it had finished its cycle. "I'm going to put the towels in the dryer. You want me to get anything for you while I'm up?"

"No, I'm okay." Hugh straightened himself and rubbed his face on his sleeve as Pablo got up off of the couch. "Thanks for talking to me. I don't know how you put up with me all the time."

Pablo poked his head back into the room. "What are you talking about? I don't 'put up' with you. I love you."

"You say that, but it can't be easy."

"It's really not as bad as you think it is."

Hugh gripped his hair in his hands. "Why are you so perfect? It's driving me insane!"

Pablo laughed. "I am *far* from perfect."

"You're always so kind. You never complain. You just go with the flow. I'm so jealous."

"You know, sometimes you give off that impression. Not to me, of course—I know you—but to others. I bet you'd be less stressed if you opened up a little more." Pablo started the dryer and returned to the couch. "I know we've talked about this before, but have you thought about *actually* talking to your therapist?"

Hugh scoffed. "I don't need that. It's just a box they check so I can keep doing my job. Everyone would think I was a joke."

"First of all, not everyone has to know. But more importantly, you know full well how common that actually is. Everybody needs some help sometimes. Even—no, *especially*—the helpers."

Hugh, of course, knew that. There had been many times in his career path where he had been recommended to therapists. But there was no time, and he simply did not want to go. What would his coworkers think? His patients? And his husband, oh, sweet Pablo already put up with enough without his husband being *actually* in therapy. There was no need to add more strain to their relationship. And Hugh didn't want anyone thinking he was weak. He'd already been there with his dad—there was no reason to go through it again. So he tried not to think about it.

"If we had a kid, who would do their laundry?" he asked, changing the subject.

Pablo sighed in frustration, but couldn't keep from laughing, too. "Me, of course! You'd turn all their clothes pink."

It's All Made Up

There were three seconds left on the clock. George dribbled the ball down the court, the coarse rubber sliding against his hand as the ball bounced off the shining wood floor. There were two players in red jerseys between him and the game-winning shot--the lanky redhead with braces, and the short guy with the afro that made him look nearly as tall as his teammate. Knowing the second player was mostly hair, George ducked in that direction and then leapt up into the air, launching the ball toward the basket.

"Nothin' but net! And it's another win for George Wong and Riverside High!" the announcer's voice boomed from the gym speakers. The crowd on the nicer bleachers, all dressed in royal blue, erupted into cheers. On the other side of the gym, red-shirted parents and friends cursed under their breath.

A blur of blue came together in the middle of the court, with George hoisted up to the top of a mob of sweaty boys. Amidst the overpowering odor of teenage bodies and the feeling of all the warm, wet arms lifting him into the air, he beamed, and his teammates rejoiced.

Once the cheering and commotion died down, the Coach Rancis had his say, the boys gathered in the locker room to pack up all of their stuff. Hakeem approached George.

"Hey, man, a bunch of us are headed to Pizza Hut. You in?" Behind Hakeem, Juan and Harrison, the typical drivers, were pulling out their keys and wallets.

"Ah, I wish I could, but you know how my parents are," George said.

Juan rolled his eyes. "See, told you he wouldn't come."

Hakeem groaned. "Come on, man! It's senior year!"

"You should at least ask," Harrison said. "You never know."

George sighed. "Alright, I'll ask. But don't get your hopes up."

Back in the gym, George's parents--along with his brother Vincent, who was on his phone, and his sister Lily, who was chatting with a friend--stood like statues by the main exit doors. Most of the other parents were talking amongst themselves or congratulating their kids. But as George approached, his parents did nothing of the sort.

"Do you have everything to study for your math test tomorrow?" Mrs. Wong asked.

"Yes, it's all in my backpack." George shuffled his feet nervously. "But, Mom, I was wondering, can I go out for dinner with the guys tonight? Either Juan or Harrison will be driving me, and I will have them drop me off at home by eleven."

"And where will you be going?"

"Pizza Hut."

"To study?"

"No, Mom, just to eat dinner and hang out. Celebrate winning the game."

"Absolutely not," Mr. Wong said. "You need to go home and study, or you'll never get into a good college."

George rolled his eyes. "I don't think hanging out with friends *one time* is going to ruin my chances of going to college."

"Don't you roll your eyes at us young man!" His mother's cheeks grew red. "We are going home right this instant, and you are going to study and go to bed by ten."

George turned around to tell his teammates the news, but they had already turned away and started walking toward the other exit.

George was five years old on that June day when the Wong family first made their fortune and moved into the big white house on the hill. Vincent was three. Lily had just turned one.

Mrs. Wong was excited about entertaining friends and family in the home in the evenings. Mr. Wong liked how the house looked out over the town, sitting pretty on that grassy hill in the best part of the suburbs. Both parents looked forward to being admired by everyone who did *not* live in a big white house on a hill. George, however, cared for none of that. While his father was gone at work and his mother directed movers, designers, and artists around the home, he and his little brother raced up and down the long, empty halls, sliding on the polished wood floor in their socks. After three laps of the highest floor, they would scoot down the stairs on their bums and sneak into their father's office, the first room in the house to be fully furnished. The two boys rummaged through the desk drawers until they found highlighters and blank printer paper, and then set to coloring on the floor, their small bodies lying on the brand-new Persian rug that dominated the room and their papers pressed by grubby hands against the dark wood floors.

"Look! A dragon!" Vincent held up his paper, his round cheeks raised to his eyes in a smile. On the page was a blur of neon green. "Roar!"

George clutched his own paper and giggled with delight as his brother chased him around the room. Then he stopped abruptly and turned to face his brother. "Stay back, dragon! I'm here to slay you!" He turned his paper around to reveal a boxy blue man with a long blue line—a sword—in his blobby hand.

"You will never get to the princess!" Vincent took off running out of the room, followed closely by George.

The two boys entered the nursery, with its baby pink walls covered with floral wall-sticker designs. The white crib under the window contained Lily, the littlest Wong, in a lilac onesie accented with a felt tiara on the chest. She smiled and sat up when she saw her brothers.

Vincent stood in front of the crib, holding out his dragon, roaring. George ran up to him and tackled him to the plush gray carpet under their feet, tickling him as he kicked and laughed. Lily squealed excitedly as she watched the boys wrestle on the floor. Soon, George the knight stood up, the victor over Vincent the dragon, and tickled his baby sister through the bars of her crib. That was when their mother arrived.

She stood in the doorway, hand on her hip. "George! Vincent! What are you doing?"

"We're just playing, Mommy," George said.

Lily started crying.

"See, now, look what you've done! Disturbing your baby sister." Mrs. Wong rushed over to the crib and picked up her daughter, cradling her in her arms. "And you shouldn't be playing right now anyway. You both have school work to do. Don't you want to be successful?"

"We did it all already," Vincent said.

Mrs. Wong raised an eyebrow. "You did?"

The boys nodded.

"So if I go back into your rooms and check your math books, the whole thing will be done?"

They nodded again.

"Okay, I'm going right now to check. You better be telling the truth." She turned to leave.

George looked at his brother. "Did you do the whole book?"

Vincent shook his head. "You?"

George did the same.

Both boys went barreling out of the nursery and beat their mother to their bedrooms. They spent the rest of that summer evening apart, working diligently in their math workbooks long after sunset.

George sat on his bed in his room one Wednesday afternoon, AP U.S. Government textbook open to his left, laptop in front of him with a Google Document of notes shared with a couple of classmates pulled up and YouTube tab minimized, calculator and AP Calculus notebook to his right. Pencils, erasers, and eraser shavings covered the right side of the bed, while his just-washed basketball uniform lay under the government book on the left. In his lap was the syllabus for the psychology course he was taking through the local community college, and behind him, on the pillows, were *Hamlet* and a printed list of colleges with medical schools his father had given him to look at.

Somewhere on the bed, George's phone vibrated. He lifted up his books and rummaged through the pillows until he found it just under the top of the comforter. He had a text from Hakeem: **Hey man, party at my place Friday night, Mom's out of town. You in?**

You know my parents will never let me go, George replied.

Just ask.

Why should I bother?

It took Hakeem a moment to respond. **Rosamel will be there.**

Idk man. She hadn't been in school for weeks. Would it be worth it?

Come and don't tell your folks.

George sighed. You know they track my location on my phone.

Leave the phone there.

What if they come in to check on me and I'm not here? Beads of sweat formed at George's hairline. I'll be dead.

Look man, I keep trying to help you out. The other guys, they been talking. I can't keep defending you.

Then don't.

George threw his phone across the room, wincing as it smashed into his closet doors. It didn't break, somehow, he saw when he got off the bed to check on it. He texted Hakeem again: **Sorry man. I'll ask my parents, but don't get your hopes up.**

As the family sat down for dinner that night—a meal prepared by their personal chef, Dinah, as per usual—George asked his parents if he could hang out with Hakeem that Friday night. They, as anticipated, said no.

"Don't you know where that boy is from? You can never be seen in that part of town," Mrs. Wong said as she took a bite of her salad.

George had been about to take a bite of his salad as well, but he put his fork down. "He's my best friend, Mom. Don't talk like that."

"Regardless," Mr. Wong interjected, "you need to keep up with your studies. Friday night is the best night to get work done because everyone else will be busy and you won't have these...distractions."

"It's my senior year. I want to have a little fun."

"Senior year is what makes or breaks your future. You need to keep your grades up," Mr. Wong said. "Or, if you don't want to study, or look at colleges, practice basketball. Or tennis–it's been a while since you've been out on the tennis court. I bet Alejandro will be available tomorrow if you want a lesson."

"No, Dad, I don't want a tennis lesson, and I don't want to practice basketball, and I don't want to apply for colleges, and I don't want to study–none of that on a Friday night! I want to see my friends!"

Mrs. Wong slammed her fist on the table, silencing George and his father. "We said no. That's final. Now hurry up and eat so we can get Lily to her dance recital." She looked down the table to her daughter and smiled.

Lily smiled back quickly, then continued eating her food.

George stood up abruptly. "Shouldn't I be allowed to go do something fun? All the teachers, the doctors, and the government have been talking about the importance of mental health this year and last, and you never take it seriously."

"It's because there is nothing to take seriously. It's all made up," Mr. Wong said. "Now sit back down and finish your dinner." He looked his son in the eyes sternly. "Now."

George sat, and he said nothing more about Hakeem. He would spend that Friday night writing college application essays.

George tested out of Biology 101 and 102 because of his AP scores from high school, but there were many moment in which he wished he hadn't. One of those was a Wednesday morning sitting in BIO 211, listening to his weathered old professor drone on and on about human anatomy. Or maybe it was genetic diseases. The days ran together from the beginning of the course. Even on the days when George couldn't pull himself out of bed to go to class, he sat on his computer gazing hopelessly at PowerPoint slides. On this particular day, he did go to class, though he wished he hadn't. He wore the same sweatpants and t-shirt he'd worn since the previous Wednesday, and he didn't bring his textbook. He barely remembered to grab the key to his dorm room.

After class, the professor–what was his name again?-- called George up to the room. "George," he said, "one of the benefits of being in the Honors program is small class sizes. Smaller classes mean stronger connections with students. I hope I'm not overstepping here–I've noticed you skipping class a lot, and you don't look like you've been eating much, so I just wanted to check in to make sure you were okay."

George blinked a few times to keep the professor in focus. "Uh, yeah, I'm fine. Just stressed, that's all."

"College is a stressful time for many students, so I understand that. It's just...are you sure there is nothing else going on? We're only halfway through the semester, so there's time to turn things around. I'm happy to share some resources with you that I think would help, like tutoring and counseling. We have tutors through the university, and we have a partnership with a few different medical practices in town."

George scoffed. "You think I'm crazy?"

The professor blushed a little. "No, not at all. I think you're human. We all need a little help sometimes, you know. There's no shame in that."

"I was valedictorian in high school. Straight A's my whole life." George's heart was racing. " MVP in tennis and runner-up in basketball. I don't need *help*. I'll work harder, I promise."

"Work harder? George, you don't look like you could possibly work any harder. You need to take care of yourself—take a shower, get out in the sun, have a nice full meal." The professor's blue eyes glowed with concern. "I really think you should consider looking into some of those resources. Particularly counseling."

George didn't respond.

"Tell you what," the professor said, "I'm going to send you an email with a list of resources. It's up to you whether or not you look at them. You can delete the email as soon as you get it if you want. But I really think you should consider some of this."

George went back to his dorm immediately after class. He climbed into bed and hid under the covers to cry, as he usually did that time of day. Normally he felt a little lighter after a good cry, so long as no one saw him. But this time, every tear that fell was like a brick added on to his back. Everything felt heavy. So he cried harder, trying to make the weight go away. "You're stronger than this," he said to himself between sobs. But he only cried louder, and then the day became a blur. He had no memory of going into the bathroom for a razor, no memory of his blood running down the shower drain, no memory of his roommate coming in and screaming and calling 911.

All that George would remember of that day was the conversation with his unnamed biology professor and waking up in a bright white room to the smells of lemon and bleach, alone in a papery blue gown.

The high school auditorium was packed full–no, over-full–of friends and families of the theater, all bundled up in their hats and gloves and scarves and thick coats. Lily had texted George last week and told him about the theater performance and that she hoped he would come, if he could. She knew she'd been in the hospital a while, she'd said, but it would mean a lot to her if he could make it.

George wanted to go, of course. Vincent and Lily had always come to his games–why shouldn't he go to big events for them too? Even though they only went to his because their parents made them, he wanted to show his support. Especially for Lily. She was the only person in the family who'd kept in contact with him the last couple of months. That was the dilemma: he knew his parents wouldn't want to see him, and if Vincent had his way he wouldn't even be at the show. Regardless, he was sure to have his phone in his hand.

George slipped in just as the volunteer ushers–his old English teacher and a couple of seniors he barely recognized

–closed the auditorium doors and escorted someone's great grandparents to their seats. The lights were dim, and while the theater teacher went on and on about how much work the freshman students had been putting into this year's performance of *Romeo and Juliet*, he scanned the back rows for a seat and the front rows for his family. The Wongs, of course, always had seats reserved near the stage. Only three, now, though. He'd been practically disowned.

Finding nowhere to sit, he settled for leaning against the back wall with the divorced dads who almost didn't find out about the performance in time and the overworked moms who arrived at the exact last minute they could. George had never associated with them before, but looking around, he saw they were not quite so different from himself. They did all come alone.

When Lily had texted him about the show, and told him what play they were performing, he of course asked what part she played. Not being a major theater person, she had a relatively small part, but being the youngest child of the wealthiest family in town, she had a part nonetheless. She was playing Lady Montague, and her death scene was re-vised so that she would have a solo dance to dramatize it and to give her more stage time, as her mother requested. Lily was not supposed to know all of this, she said to her brother, but she had overheard her mother on the phone one night earlier in the semester. George felt for Lily, and couldn't help but wonder how much of his own success up until high school graduation had been due not to his own merit but to his mother's wiles and his father's wallet.

George wondered who the rest of the cast was, and peered over the shoulder of a woman in the back row of seats–there were no more programs available when he arrived, since he had to come late to avoid his parents–to see if he recognized anyone else in the play. Romeo was being played by a boy named Nathan–could it be the same Nathan that Lily mentioned she had a crush on a few weeks back? He would have to keep an eye out to see. Jamari, who Lily talked about all the time as being one of the best actors she had ever seen, was playing Mercutio because their teacher let him pick whatever role he wanted and he found that one more interesting. Juliet was played by Annabeth. Lily hated Annabeth with a passion George had never seen in his younger sister before. He wondered if it had anything to do with Nathan.

After the show, George didn't dare approach the stage with the rest of the audience to congratulate the actors on an excellent performance. It *was* excellent, there was no disputing that, but he didn't want to run into his parents, who he knew would be the first to see his sister. He texted her instead: **Hey, great job tonight. Will I get to see you at all?**

Then he watched the crowds. Lily was still on stage, and so were his parents. They were talking. When Lily excused herself to go backstage, they followed. When the three of them came back out a couple minutes later, Mr. and Mrs. Wong's faces were as red as the stage curtains with anger. Lily's face was so covered in stage makeup that George couldn't tell what she was feeling. He did know, however, that they'd all seen his text. They were scanning the room for him.

He thought about leaving. It would be easy to duck out then, to run across the street to the music store parking lot, get into his car, and drive back to the hospital. Check himself back in—the nurses knew who he was, it wouldn't be much trouble. He could be safely in a room before his parents found him, and he could tell the nurses not to let them up. If they even bothered to follow him; perhaps they would just let him go and pretend it never happened. But George didn't want that to be how the night ended. He hadn't seen his sister in months. He wanted to congratulate her on her performance in person, to hug her and tell her how proud he was. So he walked toward the stage, weaving through the other family members there to see their young actors perform, keeping his eyes on his family the whole time so that when they did see him, they'd know he was ready.

"How dare you show your face here," Mr. Wong said once George was with his family. Vincent, too, was standing there, but he had the hood of his sweatshirt up over his head and was playing on his phone, not paying attention.

"I came to see Lily." George turned to his sister and smiled. "You did great tonight, sis. I'm really glad I got to see you."

She hugged him. "Thanks for coming."

With one hand, Mrs. Wong grabbed her daughter's arm and yanked her back; with the other, she picked at the skin around her cuticles. "Lily! Get away from him!" She then regained her composure, straightening her back. "We don't associate with people like him."

"*People like him?*" Lily asked, turning to face her mother. "He's my brother!"

"Not anymore he's not." Mr. Wong had yet to look George in the eye, and that did not change. He turned to Vincent. "Vincent, go get the car. We are leaving. Now."

Vincent rolled his eyes and walked toward the auditorium doors, never looking up from his phone.

"No son of mine is a college drop-out," Mr. Wong continued.

"I got sick!" George threw his hands in the air. "I would have failed every class if I hadn't dropped them all. And I had to take care of myself."

"*Sick*, yeah right. All of this pandemic nonsense," Mrs. Wong said. "It's been nearly two years. I don't think it ever really existed. People are just getting lazy, and weak."

"Precisely." Mr. Wong stepped beside his wife. "Success takes hard work, pushing through when times get tough. Not checking into a hospital when you feel sad." He shook his head. "Pathetic."

George felt tears welling up in his eyes, but he held them back. "I didn't come here to be chastised. I came to see my sister perform in her play. And I did, so I'm leaving." He turned to Lily. "I'm so sorry, sis. You really did great tonight." And then he left. As he walked away, he heard his sister and parents get into a fight.

"How could you treat him like that? He's really trying. Everyone at school says the pandemic *is* real, and you can see it, right there in George," Lily said.

"What we can *see* is that our eldest is weak, and a failure." Mrs. Wong huffed. "I don't understand why he came back to embarrass our family."

Lily raised her voice. "He didn't come back to embarrass anyone! He came back to support me!"

"You don't need the support of someone like that," Mr. Wong said. "That's what family is for."

"George *is* family!" Tears were streaming down Lily's cheeks, George knew, just as they streamed down his. He and his sister were alike in that way. "Vincent, say something!" she cried.

The cacophony of proud parents and energetic young actors. George thought, was by far preferable to the shouting of his family and parents.

George awoke to *Star Wars'* R2D2 beeping at him from his phone. It was 2 a.m. Only two people could bypass his nighttime "Do Not Disturb" settings, and it was a groupchat with both of them that woke him.

The message was from Lily. **We're on our way. Don't ask questions, we'll explain when we get there.**

George groaned and rolled onto his stomach, faceplanting into his pillow. Then he shot up. What did they mean, they were on their way? Not just Lily, but Vincent, too? It had been months since George had talked to Vincent. His younger brother hadn't said a word to him at Lily's performance a few weeks back.

ETA? George replied.

It didn't take long for Lily to respond. **3:30.**

They must have just left. George scrambled out of bed and looked around his apartment. A heads-up would have been nice, but he knew sometimes that wasn't possible. Something must have happened at home. George laughed to himself as he pulled a pair of gray sweatpants over his boxers. *Home.* What a concept. That town hadn't been home to him in a long time, if it ever really had been. He imagined his siblings felt the same. What he couldn't imagine, however, was what would have brought them to him in the middle of the night. Or how they even got out of the house, with all of the security cameras and alarms. Once he was dressed and had tidied up the apartment a little,

George pulled some pancake mix out of the cabinet and put a skillet on the stove. He didn't know if they would be hungry or not, but better safe than sorry. Lily was always in a bad mood when she was hungry.

No one said a word when Vincent and Lily arrived at George's apartment. George helped his younger siblings carry their suitcases up the stairs to the second floor and got them settled in. Vincent would sleep on the floor, and Lily on the couch. George wished he had more to offer them, but his dated studio could only provide so much. He was lucky to even have a place—his maintenance job at the hospital near his old college paid just barely enough for him to get by.

The three Wong children sat down on the floor of George's living space and ate bland, imperfectly cooked pancakes with their hands off of paper plates.

"I'm pregnant," Lily said abruptly. She dropped her fork, but didn't look up from her plate.

Lily? Pregnant? Every big brother instinct in him was ready to kill somebody, but he held back, taking slow, deep breaths. That wasn't what she needed.

"How long?" he asked after a time.

"Six weeks."

"She told me as soon as she found out," Vincent said. "That was, what, Tuesday?"

Lily nodded, and then burst into tears. Vincent held her against him.

"So it's only been a couple days. We weren't going to tell Mom and Dad, of course, but then last night they saw the pregnancy test in the trash." Vincent sighed. "All hell broke loose, as I'm sure you can imagine."

"They wanted me to get an abortion!" Lily cried.

"And you don't want to?" George asked.

She shook her head, still racked with sobs.

"They said if she didn't abort, they would kick her out," Vincent said. "I...I couldn't let that happen. I told them they were being cruel. So they threatened to kick me out too. And, well...here we are." He took a breath. "I've been saving up money from my computer business for the last couple of years. The plan was to save up enough to move out of the country and never come back, but...I want to use it to help pay rent and take care of Lily's baby. It's only a couple thousand dollars, but I'll keep working and saving up more."

George felt tears welling up in his eyes, not with sadness because his siblings were disowned as he had been—though he felt awful for them, of course—but with pride. Vincent, who had been passively letting things happen in their household since he was a little kid, stood up for their baby sister. Vincent and Lily both had learned to stand up for themselves, too, and they did so long before George ever could. And here they all were, together in one place. George wrapped both Vincent and Lily in a big hug, and they all cried together. "I'm so proud of you both. It's going to be hard, but we'll get through all of this. Together. As a family"

Retrospect

When Nazira first got her job as a mail carrier, there was no one more excited for her than Harold.

"You're gonna get us out of here, sis," he said.

She turned around from the kitchen sink, hands dripping with soapy water. "I don't make all that much. And I won't get us anywhere, not for years."

He rolled his eyes. "You have a job. That's more than I can say, and more than Ma or Pa could say. Be proud."

"Don't talk like that," she snapped. She then turned back to the dishes.

"Don't be proud of you?" He laughed. "You're ridiculous. Now move over, I'll do the dishes. You're a working woman now—let me take care of stuff here."

"You're the one being ridiculous. Now get off my back so I can finish these and make dinner."

Nazira lay in the hospital bed, staring up at the white tile ceiling, driving her gaze along the lines between the tiles. She stopped every so often, getting out of Scar Face with a stack of paper mail and a package or two for delivery. She walked up the steps to the Johnson home and watched the kids running around inside, their wearied father sitting in the hall with his hands on his head.

"Ms. Adebimpe?"

Nazira turned her head slightly to the door. Dr. Corbrum stood in the doorway, clipboard in hand.

"How are we feeling today?" he asked.

"I need to get back out there." Tears formed in her eyes. "No one else will deliver to Hazelwood."

Dr. Corbrum sighed. "We've talked about this. Remember what we said yesterday?"

Nazira's sigh was far deeper than her doctor's. "I have to focus on me. I know. But there's nothing to focus on. I'm nothing without my truck, without my job. I was the only one in my family to get a real job, did you know that?"

He nodded. "Yes, you told me that. And as I said before, you are putting a lot of pressure on yourself. I'm surprised you went as long as you did before seeking help."

"I didn't *seek* anything. I passed out in the truck and someone brought me in."

"Ah, yes, I remember."

"I just wanna go back to work."

"I know, but you can't, Nazira. You're still sick."

"I'm not sick."

"You are." Dr. Corburm sat on the side of her bed. "You've been here two weeks today, did you know that?"

Nazira shook her head.

"No amount of medicine I've prescribed has helped, and no amount of talk therapy has made any amount of progress toward your recovery. And I think I know why. Do you?"

She shook her head again.

"You have to *want* it, Nazira. You can't get better until you want to."

"I'm not sick, so there's nothing to want."

He sighed, and there was a profound tiredness in his hazel eyes. "Okay. I'm going to send Dr. Allen in here again to talk to you for a bit. Please try to talk to her today, alright?"

Nazira rolled her eyes and turned away from the psychiatrist. She didn't want to see her therapist. Not that day, not ever. She didn't need it. She didn't need anything but her routine and her job. That's how she'd made it so far into the pandemic without getting sick–focusing on her work. If she hadn't fainted in front of the Vanderbilt home, she wouldn't be in the hospital and she wouldn't be on forced leave. She hadn't eaten enough that day, that was all.

Harold refused to go to the hospital. He didn't need it, he couldn't afford it, he didn't want to take a bed from someone else–there were a variety of reasons, some of them understandable, for his resistance to treatment. When he died, he collapsed in his deceased friend Dayvon's kitchen, at the sink, wet sponge in one hand and stained plastic plate in the other.

Nazira wanted to hold a funeral for him. But who would come? All of his friends had already passed into the next world–she hoped Heaven, but it was hard to say, really–and there was no family left but her. He had no money, and she couldn't pay for it by herself. She'd been due for a raise for months, but because of the pandemic it was put on hold. So there was no funeral. When his body was cremated, Nazira kept his ashes in the tin they came in, planning to take them to the cemetery once the ground was warm enough to bury them. Harold would sit on her TV stand for years.

It had been one month since Nazira was admitted to the psych floor of the hospital. She had seen many patients come and go, including many on her mail route. Both daughters of Penelope Solay, the eldest Wong child, and a handful of Johnsons all came and went. Dr. Corbrum was off work on paternity leave that week, so it was just her therapist and the nurses checking in on her.

"Hi Nazira, how are you doing?" Dr. Allen asked.

"I'm okay, I guess." Nazira propped herself up in the bed. "A little tired."

The therapist sat in a chair opposite the bed. "Do you mean physically tired, like sleepy, or emotionally tired?" she asked, pen in hand and notebook on her lap.

"Both, maybe."

"Any idea why you're feeling tired?"

"I just want to go home."

Dr. Allen smiled. "I know, I know. You've made some good progress in the last couple weeks, so I think that will happen very soon." She looked down at her notes. "Any weird dreams last night?"

"Yeah, but it wasn't as bad as Monday or Tuesday. Is that good?"

"Maybe. But bad dreams come and go with stress. The worse ones may come back, and if they do, that doesn't necessarily mean you are doing something wrong."

"Can I go back to work, when I'm out?" Nazira asked.

Dr. Allen sighed. "I think you should take some more time off. Let yourself rest and recover at home for a while."

"I don't think they'll let me."

"Really? Even in light of the pandemic?"

"That's over, everybody says." Nazira looked straight at Dr. Allen. "It *is* over, right?"

"Something like this," the therapist said, "never really ends, not without major institutional and societal change. We've certainly taken steps in the right direction in the past couple years, but what you said about work not letting you take more time off? That indicates to me that there is still a major problem." She closed her notebook and placed it and her pen on the floor. "You aren't a machine, Nazira. People aren't machines. We need rest, and fun, and community, and joy. You can't keep working yourself into the ground. You go back to work as soon as you're released from here, you'll find yourself right back in this bed. Maybe not right away, but you will. And I think you know that."

Nazira nodded solemnly. "Yeah, I know." She turned away to gaze out the window. "But I don't have anything else."

Nazira sat at her usual table—the round, broken one in the corner of the cafeteria—with Charlene, Maryah, and Nirupa. Four plastic trays with rectangular pizzas, bland mashed potatoes, and chocolate milk cartons adorned the table's chipped surface.

"I can't wait until your birthday, Char," Maryah said, twirling a plastic fork in her pile of beige mush. "Once you can drive, we're getting out of here."

Charlene sighed. "Just because I'll be 16 doesn't mean I'll have a car. You know my daddy can't afford it—hell, he can barely pay for his own."

"A nice thought, though, leaving this place. I'd give any-thing." Nazira hadn't even touched her lunch, and had no intention of doing so. "If we were to go anywhere, be any-thing, what would you guys want to do?"

Nirupa spoke up first. "I'd go to med school, become a doctor. Of course, that's not likely to happen."

"This isn't about what's *gonna* happen, it's about what we want." Charlene scratched her head. "I really want to be a mom. Show my kids something better than what I got."

Nazira scoffed. "You can do that anyway. Don't you want to be something else?"

"No. But I don't want to stay here. I want to get out to the suburbs–go on stroller jogs with the other mamas, and cook dinner for my rich hubby." Charlene winked.

Maryah laughed forcibly. "You and marrying rich. You're pretty enough, at least. I'll be lucky to marry at all."

"Don't talk like that," Charlene said.

"Yeah, you're very pretty," Nazira added.

Maryah rolled her eyes. "Whatever. Marrying wouldn't be my dream, anyway. I want to be a famous skater. Show off my tricks on the TV."

Nirupa smiled. "That would be cool!"

"What about you, Naz?" Charlene asked. "What would you be?"

The sun sat high in the sky, looking lovingly down on the world it grew. It sat in a circle of tree tops, a sea of baby blue, pillows of white. And Nazira sat surrounded by great tree trunks, in a meadow of wavy green speckled with yellow and white and pink. She had not been to this clearing since she was a little girl, but when she plopped down on the dewy grass, she felt as though it had been waiting to hold her all her life.

She lay back and closed her eyes, listening to the chirping of the birds around her. They sounded so happy and free, singing their little melodies to their hearts' content. Somewhere in the distance, children laughed and played, frolicking through the trees like she and Harold did when she was young. She remembered Ma screaming after them to come back and get their coats, Pa calling them in for dinner as the sun began to set. The woods behind Hazelwood were a natural playground, a kingdom wilderness hers for the claiming. And as she lay in her favorite clearing so many years later, Nazira knew that her kingdom had been lost. But when? Perhaps she lost it when Ma died of cancer no one would treat, or when Pa drank himself to death. Perhaps it was when Harold had to drop out of school at 17 to care for her. Or maybe it was when she got that job as a mail carrier just after her twenty-second birthday and suddenly she was better than all the things that came before. Nazira never thought that way, but Harold did, and so did all their friends and neighbors. She was too good. She was going to up and leave and never return. To Harold, that was a dream. To others, a betrayal.

Nazira reached into her jacket pocket and pulled out her phone. She scrolled through her contact list, skimming through names of people she might have called ten years ago. She really wasn't sure why she still had their numbers, or if any of the numbers would still work. She didn't know if any of them were still alive, really. So she looked to Facebook instead and cried as she saw the happy lives led by the people she once considered friends–family, even. Some of them worked; some of them didn't. And though she knew social media was never a fully accurate picture of a person's life, she also knew that these people *had* lives. If she lost her own, no one would notice.

If she never returned to work, would anyone mourn?

Without another moment's hesitation, Nazira dialed her boss's number and quit, smiling as her boss went on and on about how he should have fired her earlier, how she is lucky to even have the job, how she shouldn't expect to use him as a reference for anything. She hung up the phone and tossed it onto the grass. She was free.

As she watched the birds overhead, Nazira marveled at the possibilities that lay out in the world, hers for the taking. She could go anywhere, do anything. Maybe she would go to school to be a teacher, or a doctor, even. Maybe she would travel the world. She had no connections in that town anymore, nothing tying her down. It would be lonely for a while, sure. But she would be lonely forever if she did nothing. So she stood up from the ground, brushing the grass off her jeans, and left to claim the life she had been given.

Cas Luthman is a student at the University of South Carolina studying to get her Masters in Teaching for English. She graduated from the University of South Carolina in May of 2022 with a Bachelor of Arts in English and a Minor in Sociology. Before starting college in Columbia, SC, she spent her childhood in West Liberty, OH and her teenage years in New Bern, NC. She has been writing fiction as long as she can remember and loves to write speculative fiction, science fiction, and fantasy.